DARKNESS

Brandon Faircloth

Dedicated to my mother--a wonderful writer, teacher, and friend.

Other Works by Brandon Faircloth:
Mystery
On the Hill and Other Tales of Horror
Whimsical Leprosy
The Outsiders: Book One (Coming Soon)
You Saw Something You Shouldn't Have (Coming Soon)

I found a dimpled spider, fat and white,
On a white heal-all, holding up a moth
Like a white piece of rigid satin cloth--
Assorted characters of death and blight
Mixed ready to begin the morning right,
Like the ingredients of a witches' broth--
A snow-drop spider, a flower like a froth,
And dead wings carried like a paper kite.

What had that flower to do with being white,
The wayside blue and innocent heal-all?
What brought the kindred spider to that height,
Then steered the white moth thither in the night?
What but design of darkness to appall?--
If design govern in a thing so small.

Design by Robert Frost

...The waves were dead; the tides were in their grave,
The Moon, their mistress, had expired before;
The winds were withered in the stagnant air,
And the clouds perished; Darkness had no need
Of aid from them--She was the Universe.

Darkness by Lord Byron

Prologue

"Juxtaposition, Harold. That's the key."

Harold Chambry stifled another yawn as he sat in the Major's tent, his eyes grainy with fatigue. He had been up for nearly two days, and the only thing he could think of was sleep. They were only a mile back from the front trenches, forty-five miles west of Berlin. The artillery fire was an accepted constant after three weeks, and he found himself looking out through the tent's narrow opening when it stopped momentarily, a lost look upon his face.

"Juxtaposition."

Harold turned back to find Major Stalling watching him intently, a mild irritation at his lack of interest apparent in the set of the older man's mouth as he rolled a toothpick from one side to the other.

"Juxtaposition, sir?"

"Yes, Sergeant. The intersection of the old and the new, the familiar and the strange, the light and the dark." The officer leaned back in his chair and smiled expansively, as if his words carried some great significance or weight. The only thing that Harold could focus on with any clarity at this point was that the Major wasn't using the word 'juxtaposition' right. Deciding it would be unwise to correct his superior officer, he nodded, hoping it was all the response that was required. It was.

"We only see things from our tiny perspective, you see. We stumble through life clueless. Never comprehending or seeing the signs."

"Signs? Signs of what, sir?" God, he wanted sleep. His clothes were so dirty they were a part of him, and while he couldn't hope for a bath, he could at least take a nap. If this torture ever ended.

"Signs of what. That is the question, isn't it? But the answer to that is beyond you, I'm afraid. All I can do is point you to the signs themselves." The man leaned closer, the sour smells of whiskey and sweat coming across the distance as he continued. "A man misses a turn and winds up at a diner where he meets the love of his life. A child trips and gets run over by a car. The woman that ran him over? The daughter of the couple from the diner, all grown up. The death of that child then causes the suicide of his father, which leads to his wife winding up in the arms of another man...and so on. And that is just using love and death as examples. But it *all* matters. It *all* serves a purpose. There is no coincidence. Every event is part of a greater pattern. A sprawling design that stretches across all of existence."

Harold shifted uncomfortably in his seat, his mind grown sharper as the strangeness of the Major's words set in. He had never loved being under Major

Stalling's command, what with him being a pompous ass and all, but the man had never spoken like this before.

"Major, I..."

"I had a dream last night, Harold. More than a dream, really. An awakening. I saw some part of this vast pattern, glimpsed the edge of its rhyme and reason. And I understood immediately the role I must play in all of this."

"What do you mean?"

The Major stood, his eyes glassy as he looked down at Harold. "I was supposed to go home six months ago, Sergeant. Did you know that? Medical leave, they were calling it. But then *my* superior officer took a bullet in the head, and suddenly I was too valuable to let go. So I was made to stay. And then you came under my command. Now I understand why."

Stalling pulled out the service revolver smoothly, the expression on his face never changing. Harold sat back quickly when he registered the gun, almost rising before thinking better of it.

"You were only a mediocre soldier, Harold, but I am sorry this is necessary. If only there was more time to make you understand."

In that moment, Harold knew he was going to die. He accepted it easily, not out of courage, but simply because he saw no way to avert it. He fumbled for a prayer even as the Major's neck snapped.

As the Major fell to the ground, the figure behind him came into view. He was a short man in a crisp white suit, his features so plain as to fade from Harold's memory the moment he looked back down at Stalling's prone form. When he looked back up, the man had taken a step closer, his face unsmiling. When the man spoke, his voice was barbed wire in Harold's brain.

"You have been given a great gift today, Mr. Chambry. Do you believe that?"

"Y-yes."

"Good. As with everything, this gift is not free. You will have to do something to repay this kindness. Correct?"

Harold nodded mutely, a stain spreading on the front of his pants.

"Then this is what you will do." The man leaned forward and whispered, his eyes black and shining. When he was finished, he stepped back towards the shadows, pausing as Harold spoke hoarsely.

"Who are you?"

Smirking, the man nodded slightly before answering. "Do you honestly think any answer I would give you would have any truth or significance for you? Go live your life, Harold." With that, he stepped into the dark and was gone.

Harold sat shaking for several minutes, listening to the thunder of war outside as he tried to make sense of what had happened. He jumped as he heard footsteps pass by the tent. He had to find a way out of this. He had to get home.

Part I: Juxtaposition

Chapter One

Eric Talbot was born on the evening of the summer solstice at just before ten at night, as the last of the light reluctantly crept from the sky to be replaced by starlight and the thin haze of the city's pollution and ambient luminescence. His birth was unremarkable, with no complications or ordeals, and no claps of thunder or earthquakes to signify his arrival.

Which is not to say it went unnoticed. To the cluster of family in the waiting room, awaiting the arrival of their newest member, it was a very important night. Harold Chambry prayed for his daughter's safety as well of that of his first grandson, and Michael Talbot alternated between asking his own parents worried questions and pacing distractedly, cursing his decision to stay outside of the delivery room.

It is also not to say that Eric's birth had no effect upon the world. The night the boy was born, there were seven violent deaths in Atlanta, scattered over six different parts of the city. One was a wife beaten too enthusiastically by her husband, while two of the deaths were the cause of an impromptu murder-suicide of a single father and his eleven-year old daughter. All of these deaths were investigated, and there was never any serious contemplation of any connections they could have given their randomness and disparities.

Seventeen women miscarried that night in a forty-mile radius around the hospital where Eric was seeing the world for the first time, and if anyone had ever looked into it, they would have learned that all of the miscarriages happened just a few minutes before ten.

Animal Control had their hands full as well, with several dogs having to be put down due to unexpected attacks that occurred this same evening. A sweet little Pomeranian named Juju nearly bled his disabled owner to death before her weak screaming was heard.

It was as if a wave of sorrow and pain had glided in with the rising dark, washing through the streets and yards, creeping under doors and around corners. Then, just as suddenly, it was gone.

Eric Talbot was washed and given to his mother, his eyes intelligent and warm as he looked up at the sweaty but smiling woman. Unaware of all the misery, Eric took a deep breath and closed his eyes, falling fast asleep.

Secondary: The Gorgon, Part I

The air churned with dust and grit as Lawrence Hobbes scowled against the filth that had coated his face, his hair, his teeth. The taste of earth on his tongue was bitter and only punctuated the resentment he had already been feeling since he had begun work that morning.

He was to spend the summer helping his uncle run his surveying company, and in return, his oh-so-generous father would finance architect courses in the fall. Horace Hobbes had told him his terms with a wry smile, clearly disapproving of Lawrence's latest career jump. He was two months shy of his thirtieth birthday and had yet to settle on a career. Seeing as how his father refused to let him be "spoon-fed everything in life" and therefore refused to let him join the family company, Lawrence felt he had the right to take his time and find something he would actually enjoy.

This certainly wasn't it. Caught out in the middle of Kansas in the middle of a dust storm surveying land that no one in their right mind would want in the first place. He spat out a wad of brown muck and cursed his uncle again.

Lawrence was essentially a gopher. He had little to no idea of how to actually survey land, so he was reduced to toting equipment and keeping his uncle company. This afternoon, however, his doughy-faced cousin had come out to tell them that his uncle's wife had fallen and broken her leg. Dear uncle headed off with the cousin, and Lawrence was left cleaning up and eating dirt.

Closing the tailgate on the beat-up company truck, he reached into his pocket for the keys. Even as his hand slid into the pocket, he realized he wouldn't find them there.

"The fucking son of a bitch. The stupid mother fucker." Slamming his fist into the window, he screamed in rage and pain as he spun away from the webbed glass and stalked around the truck like a madman.

All of this. All of this *shit*. For what? So he could build character? Fuck his father and fuck his uncle and fuck his stupid cunts of a cousin and aunt. Fuck them all. He would...

He gasped as blackness filled his vision. This wasn't a blackout or hysterical blindness, but a midnight curtain that covered the world. All that was left was Lawrence and the cold, inky black.

The immensity of the void brought him to his knees. His brain reeled as his mouth grew pulled and slack, drool pooling against the cup of his lip and spilling over in a thick brown stream. It was so *much*.

He could have stared into that black forever, but suddenly chips of light appeared in the darkness--a slowly blossoming field of stars. Instead of being comforting or beautiful, they frightened and angered him--their light cold and imperious as they looked down upon him. He clenched his fists and was about to scream when he felt *it* coming.

It rolled in like a storm, a darkness deeper than the void and wider than the sky. It blotted out the stars one by one, devouring them as it spread. It was purer and more real than their light--than anything. Lawrence knew immediately that he had found his purpose. His god.

When he awoke, he felt unchanged except for something in the background that he could almost feel. But the changes would come with time. He had been shown what was possible. Smiling as he stood and dusted himself off, he smirked at the truck and headed out towards the road to hitch a ride.

It was only a ten minute walk, and he was whistling to himself as he walked to the shoulder of the road, his heart near bursting with the emotion raging within him. Everything was going to fall into place. Even now a delivery truck was coming down the road, speeding along as if racing to give him a ride. He chuckled to himself and stuck out his thumb, turning to give a parting glance to his uncle's truck. At least he would never have to drive that piece of shit again. Things were about to...

When the delivery truck hit him, he flew ten feet in the air before landing in a twisted heap on the asphalt. The truck was still moving however, and when his arm got caught in the delivery truck's undercarriage, he was drug another twenty feet before the squeal of brakes and the smell of burnt tires brought an end to the most important afternoon in Lawrence Hobbes' life.

Tertiary: Ritual

The air in the cave was pungent, bearing the scents of fire and earth, sweat and fear. The boy knew that some of the fear he smelled likely leaked slowly from his own skin, from his own heart. As he stood against the cool rock wall he gripped its rough surface for strength, whispering to himself. He wanted to pray, but he was afraid to do so. In this place, so far from the sun and wind, his prayers might not reach the surface, or worse, be snatched up by the thing that his uncle prayed to for hours every night.

He had been a person once. His heart had been brave and full of joy. He had been his father's only pride since his mother had grown ill, and he had loved everyone in their tribe. Then his uncle had come back from a dreamwalk that had begun years before, and when he returned he was changed. His father told him once that his uncle had once been a joyful man, full of jokes and stories for anyone who would listen. He returned with dark eyes and a brooding face that never changed, a stone against the water.

He heard the drums begin again, and his stomach seized up with such force that he slid down the wall to a sitting position, trying to make himself as small as possible as he wrapped his arms around his knees. It would begin soon, and then he could never turn back. Flames and shadows moved along the walls, dancing like evil spirits telling of his heart's demise. He trembled and thought again of what had brought him to this evil place.

Within two months of his return, the boy's uncle had swayed many with his teachings. He did so subtly, never preaching his blasphemy in the open, knowing that his brother would kill him if he heard his words. The boy knew nothing of this at the time, his only clue that something was amiss coming when his father told him to never allow himself to be alone with his uncle.

The night that his uncle stole away from the tribe, he took two dozen people with him. The boy was among them. He had been drugged, and did not wake until he was too far away to find his way back on his own. That seemed like a lifetime ago now, and at eleven, the boy felt very old. He had seen so many horrors. His uncle had claimed him as his own.

And tonight would be the closing of the circle. Tonight he would truly become his uncle's son when he took a life in the name of the Evening Star. He felt his heart quail at the thought.

"Come!" His uncle's voice rang through the chamber, his tall, dark frame just obscured from view by the curve of the tunnel. The boy rose to his feet shakily, the ceremonial knife in his hand. It's blade was made of some strange black stone--the markings carved into its surface were blasphemy to even read. His final moment was upon him. His last chance to be his father's son.

He crept up to the mouth of the tunnel, peering into the massive room that was circled by fire and dominated by a massive stone platform covered by more markings and layers of dried blood and bits of hair. He stayed close to the wall and searched out his uncle in the leaping shadows. As he expected, the man was alone, his back turned from the boy as he surveyed the altar he had made during his dreamwalk years ago. His last chance.

He knew he couldn't kill his uncle. He was too small and weak, his uncle too powerful. And he held little hope of saving his own life, or of taking it himself, as he had only this dark blade to harm himself with, and he feared it would keep his spirit if he used it. But he could still save his spirit, if he were quick and smart.

Moving silently, he crept further into the chamber, keeping tight against the shadows. He only dared to move a few feet before stopping, but it was far enough. He had found the place he had prepared.

Having snuck down into the cave two nights before, he had hollowed out a small hole underneath a spot where the rock jutted out. He knew he only had a few moments at most, and now he thrust the knife into the hollow, covering it quickly with dirt. When he was done, it looked like any other spot along the wall. He hoped it would be enough.

Making his way back to the tunnel, he felt his heart would stop at any moment. He could see what would happen next. He would go to his uncle without the knife. He would tell the man that he had hidden it and would never pray or sacrifice to the Evening Star. He would be tortured and try not to break. And then he would die.

He wanted to run, he wanted to cry, he wanted to give in. In this place more than any other, it seemed that he would be overwhelmed and that he should just stop fighting. But he remembered his father and his ancestors. He remembered who he truly was.

Standing at the edge of the tunnel again, he turned to where his uncle stood facing the center of the room. He prayed that it wasn't a trick or a trap, that his uncle truly had not seen where he had hidden the knife. If he had, his uncle would force him to use it and he would be lost.

"COME!"

He choked back a sob, but heard his wail voiced by the mewling child that lay in the center of the stone circle, the carved rock cold and hungry. Pinned by his uncle's black gaze. Food for the dark. Swallowing, he stepped forward into the firelight.

"Here, Uncle. I'm here."

Chapter Two

"Eric Talbot."

"Here."

Eric watched as Mrs. Gierrien's eyes flicked up at him for a moment before she continued to call the morning roll. There were only fourteen students in the fourth-grade class, making the roll call a little silly, but Mrs. Gierrien was a stickler for structure and tradition. She also didn't like Eric very much.

For as long as he could remember, Eric had been a good judge of character. And while that talent had never been very useful to him, it had helped him avoid people that weren't very nice. Mrs. Gierrien wasn't very nice.

Not that she was a monster or anything, because she wasn't. But she was a bitter and vindictive woman who had picked out one or two favorites at the beginning of the year and discounted the rest. Eric was not one of her favorites, but he certainly garnered a great deal of attention from her. Ronnie said that he was her 'lil' bitchboy', and as funny as that was, it was also kind of true. She would always yell at him for things that other children got away with, she would always give him the hardest and longest punishments. He was still watching her when Ronnie thumped his ear from behind.

"Hey, retard. Wake up."

Eric turned to glare at his best friend. "Watch it."

Ronnie leaned back in his desk in mock fear. "Oh, big tough guy. Going to beat me up after you're finished with Alan?"

Eric's face fell at that and the weak churning of his stomach returned. He had worried half the night and all of the morning's bus ride about this afternoon, but it had actually slipped his mind for a moment. Now that he was reminded of it, all the anxiety of what faced him flooded back.

It had all spiraled out of control so quickly. Yesterday at lunch he had been sitting with Ronnie when Shannon Murtz had fallen into his view. She had moved to their school a month before, and the rumor had quickly spread that she was a mute of some kind. She didn't break character this day either--silently crying as she gathered herself up, Alan Ricks approaching from behind her with a pleased grin spread across his face.

Alan was the smartest guy in Eric's class, extremely popular, and also one of the cruelest people he had ever met. On the surface, he appeared to simply be a bully, but upon closer examination, one realized he was much more refined than that. He was an expert at picking out people's weaknesses and exploiting them to his delight and their fear and humiliation. The fact that he was still so well-liked just confirmed for Eric that most people were very stupid.

And while Alan did enjoy to tear people down on a variety of levels, he had never considered himself above some tried and true physical violence. Exhibit A: Shannon Murtz. She had started to shuffle off, sniffling to herself as she went, never even considering responding or objecting to her treatment. Alan was about to start in on her again, watched with admiration by several of his thug friends who aspired to such acts but lacked the courage to attack a girl so openly.

"Hey, asshole. Why don't you leave her alone?" Eric regretted the words as soon as they left his mouth, but it was too late by that point. All that was left was to look as if he meant them and hope that Alan bought his bluff.

Alan rounded on him immediately, his eyes dancing as he closed the distance and brought his face down to Eric's. His voice was a threatening whisper when he spoke.

"What did you say to me, dickbreath?"

Eric paused, momentarily perplexed by the name he had been called before remembering that he had bigger fish to fry. He had to stick to his guns. Dogs could smell fear.

"You heard what I said. Leave her alone." And then, sounding lame in his own ears, "She's a girl."

Alan grinned, his eyes still bright. "So are you, but I'm still going to pound your ass into the ground."

Mrs. Gierrien had come up at that point and stopped everything, and Eric had turned to find Ronnie sitting there in stunned silence. His friend tried to convince him that it would blow over, that if he avoided Alan for a few days, he'd find a new target for his random acts of violence. But that afternoon, Alan had passed him a note that made his intentions very clear: "Tomorrow afternoon at P.E., Dickbreath."

So now he had a nickname that he didn't entirely get but that certainly wasn't positive. Worse, he was going to be beaten to a pulp in a few hours. He had never been in a fight before, but given the fact that Alan outweighed him by thirty pounds and took delight in regularly beating up other people, he knew who he would lay money on. He had seriously considered just playing sick today, but word had already spread about the impending fight. If he tried to hide from it, he'd never live it down. So now he just had to wait out the longest day of his life.

Ronnie frowned at him and hit his arm. "I'm sorry, man. I'm stupid. You'll kick his ass." He smiled weakly and without much conviction.

Eric summoned an unconvincing grin of his own. "Yeah. I'll tear him a new one."

"Get up, bitch. I'm not done with you yet."

So far the fight had not gone very well. Alan had been late to P.E., and there was a moment where hope blossomed in Eric's chest. It was very short-lived.

He had to give Alan credit, however. He was a man of his word. He had in fact pounded Eric's ass into the ground with an efficiency that belied his age. As it stood now, he was hoping that Alan would be satisfied with having knocked him to the ground and punched him in the head a couple of times. It seemed that Alan had set higher standards for himself, however.

Eric attempted to think of a comeback, but given that he had the breath knocked out of him, it was hard to focus on anything for long. And now Alan was standing over him and crouching down, preparing to pummel him again.

"I said *get up*, dickbreath."

Later on, even though far eclipsed by the seizure and the events that would follow, Eric would look at what happened next as a moment of inspiration. Because that was when he realized that Alan's crotch was in arm's reach.

Balling up a fist and flailing desperately, he was amazed when he nailed the other boy, sending him tumbling over in a gasping heap. He heard a startled breath pass through those assembled around them, other daring students who had wandered to the back of the gym to see the spectacle. He felt a dull pride at the sudden upturn in his own performance before he realized that Alan was already back up on his feet and that he was very pissed.

"I'm going to kill you, fucker." Another gasp from the audience, as 'fucker' was not used often nor typically without dire consequences. But Eric conceded that his murder would qualify as a special occasion, at least in his own eyes.

Leaping back onto Eric and knocking the breath back out of him in the process, Alan began punching and slapping him repeatedly, ignoring his best attempts to fight back and fend him off. He heard Ronnie and several others yelling for Alan to stop, their voyeuristic bloodlust changing into troubled concern at seeing one of their classmates being beaten so badly. Then suddenly it stopped and Alan was off of him.

Eric's first thought was *teacher*. But then he heard Alan screaming and he looked up to see the other boy ten feet away and grasping his right wrist. The boy looked confused as he began to cry and yell for a teacher himself. Ronnie started to help Eric up slowly even as most of the other students scattered.

Ronnie would tell Eric later that Alan had suddenly jumped off of him and hit the dirt some distance away as if he had been pushed by some unseen hand. Eric somewhat doubted that at the time, though it soon became clear to everyone that Alan was crying because his right wrist had been snapped in two. People theorized that he had thrown a bad punch and done it himself, and Eric thought the same thing for many years.

But in the end, Eric didn't remember that day for the fight or what happened to Alan as much as for what happened next. As Ronnie was helping him up, Eric began to have a seizure. His head snapped back as if he was trying to rip his own head off through sheer inertia. Crumpling to the ground, he began to make a gurgling sound even as his hands and feet curled in on themselves. Convulsing in the dirt, he didn't hear as Ronnie and others began to scream for a teacher, echoing Alan's own continued cries. He didn't remember much from the seizure itself other than a cottony feeling of disconnectedness. The world dulled and faded briefly, darkness filling the edge of his vision.

Then he sat up and heard himself speaking clearly, though he didn't understand the words or what he was seeing when he said them.

"You're going to fall."

With that, he slumped back to the ground, unconscious. When he awoke he was at home, his mother peering over him worriedly and crying when he spoke to her. He asked her later about what he had said during his seizure and she explained that his brain was probably a muddle at the time, and he may have said that because he had seen the Murtz girl fall the day before, or for any other number of reasons.

That made sense to him, but he found himself doubting it just the same. It hadn't *felt* like he was muddled in that moment. He had felt clear and strong. And it hadn't felt like he was remembering the past. It felt like he was seeing something that was going to happen. Something terrible. Some event filled with sadness and loss. Something true.

"Lawrence, we have to talk."

He gritted his teeth at the other man's words, this dottering fossil with his useless yammering, all the time in his ear. Lawrence pressed the joystick on his chair forward further, increasing his speed as George Blackwell and his son Toby struggled to keep up.

"Lawrence, just stop being an ass and listen to us." This last came from Toby, and he whipped his chair around on the words.

He took a moment to calm himself, regarding the two men before him. Clearly father and son, both were impeccably dressed in dark business suits and had the bearing of powerful men. Men who firmly grasped their destinies in their own two hands.

But that wasn't the case at all, was it? He held their futures as he held the lives of so many. And were they grateful? No, of course not. They were prattling carrion birds hoping to weary him and then pick his bones.

Not likely.

"What do you want, George? *What?*"

The older Blackwell cleared his throat, more than a little nervous now. "Well, ah, it's been some time since we've seen you in the office, Lawrence, and we..ah..."

Lawrence stabbed a finger at them, grimacing slightly at the pain it caused him. "Do you have a pussy, George? Did I crawl out of it when I was just a wee baby? Because unless that's the case, the last time I checked you weren't my fucking mother."

They were in the hallway of the executive offices, and while there weren't many staff up here, those that were fell silent during this exchange, keeping their eyes averted as they pretended to work. Let them hear it all.

George's face turned blood-red as he floundered for a response, but Toby leapt forward, pushing his face into Lawrence's. "Listen, you little gimp. You wouldn't have a pot to piss in or a window to throw it out if my father hadn't kept this company going after your old man died. So show some fucking respect or I'll shove that chair up your ass."

"Toby! That's more than enough. We're not here to argue." Giving his son a forbidding look, he turned back to Lawrence, the effort to restrain himself apparent. "Lawrence. Please just listen to what I have to say."

Lawrence leaned back in his chair, his eyes still on Toby. He'd pay for what he had said. Someday soon he'd pay. For now, he turned to the older man and feigned mild interest. "Yes?"

"Well…some of the changes you've approved these last few months. Lowering safety requirements, shipping out work to countries where they get slave labor for pennies a day….it's wrong."

"Who says? You?"

George shook his head slowly. "Your father, for one. He would never have allowed this kind of thing. He treated people as people."

"What a shame that he's dead and that I run the company now."

Toby's temper flared again. "*You* run it? *We* run it while you go running around fulfilling your sicko fantasies. We've heard all…"

"Toby, *enough!* Not another word from you."

"But Dad, you…"

"No! Nothing more." Looking at Lawrence again, "Lawrence, these changes…they're affecting the company across the board. Employee turnover is up and morale has plummeted. The products we're having produced overseas are nowhere near the level of quality our customers have come to expect. These are serious problems."

Lawrence rubbed under his nose as he studied George. Such a fat and useless man. Well, not entirely useless he supposed. The man did handle the day to day operations of the company. If not for that, he would have been fired long ago. He knew that if the Blackwells had their druthers, he would be cast aside while they stole his company right out from under him. Lawrence wasn't about to let that happen, and that meant staying in control.

"What kinds of problems, George?"

George shrugged slightly. "Take your pick. The fabric dyes we use on our clothing lines now are low-quality and fade on other clothes. We have a plant in Central America making metal furniture for us, and half of the pieces have some jagged edge or manufacture defect. We're getting mounting complaints about the wiring of our lighting fixtures. It's all reaching a boiling point."

Lawrence yawned, enjoying Troy's bristling in response. "George, are we still turning profit? Including all the potential lawsuits and loss of goodwill, when it comes down to the benefit/burden analysis, are we still making money?"

"Well yes…but don't you see that…"

"Stop right there, Georgie. That's all I needed to hear. Now quit wasting my time with this trivial bullshit. I've got an appointment to keep."

Toby wanted to say something more, but George shot him a look. It was during that momentary exchange of glances that Lawrence turned around and continued his exit out of the office. George called out to him once, but he kept on going.

Watching through the tinted windshield, Lawrence felt a quiver of excitement as he always did in the moments before a trap was sprung. This one involved a thirty-five year old banker who always took his lunch at the same time everyday. He was a family man, with two little grubs at home and a life filled with terminal mediocrity. Lawrence would give him one thing, however--he was punctual.

The man was going down the sidewalk as he always did, fifteen feet from the crosswalk. Suddenly a dark blue Impala shot across the intersection against the light, slamming into the side rear of a pickup going across, spinning it around and into the walking signal pole. The metal pole snapped and the truck slid partway onto it before drifting back down and coming to rest. But the impact and weight of the truck was enough to send the pole slamming down to the ground, hitting the family man on the way. It would have been a glancing blow if not for the force of it, hitting him on the edge of his shoulder. As it was, it ripped his right arm completely off, sending a gout of blood spraying across the concrete and several other passerby even as he collapsed to the ground. He let out one primal scream of pain as he tumbled, but then shock took over and he made no other noise aside from short huffing breaths as the life slowly leaked out of him.

Lawrence licked his lips, his eyes wide with rapturous joy as he watched it all unfold like a beautiful ballet. Even with all of the planning and preparation, they rarely went as well as this. This was a moment to be savored. He couldn't wait until later when he could watch it over and over on tape.

The drivers, tampering with the pole--everything had to be orchestrated and planned down to the last detail. This was the eighth time he had attempted to set up a death chain, and it was only the third time that it had been fully successful. He didn't know how many times he would have to do it before he received a response, if ever, but he enjoyed it nonetheless. This was what it must feel like to be God.

All done in service to that which he himself worshipped. Since that day in the field, the day of his accident, he had known that he had a great destiny. He would be the avatar for that sweeping darkness he had seen consume the stars. He simply had to recapture that which had been lost.

He knew that things had changed since his accident. The power and elation that he had felt after his epiphany had not remained when he awoke in the hospital, and he knew immediately that he must regain favor and prove himself worthy to the thing he served.

To that end, as soon as he was well enough he had begun trying to gain the attention of that darkness again. He began with prayer and meditation, but swiftly realized that was a foolish waste of time. Action was required. Then began the torture and murder of various people, all performed by bought men under Lawrence's watchful eye. The homeless, prostitutes, runaway children. All were fodder over the next few years, their lives and deaths experiments meant to shape and refine his approach. It had fulfilled that purpose to be certain, but it had also sharpened his taste for blood and pain.

It may be that he would have continued on in this fashion his entire life, but then he got an anonymous letter in the mail. He was forty by this time and head VP of the company. He had opened the letter, feeling a surge of excitement even before he read or understood it. It said: "It works by cause and effect. Patterns. So shall you."

He had attempted to have the letter traced, but to no avail. He studied the precise handwriting that formed those sentences for several days before setting out on his new plan. If that was the nature of that which he had seen, he would mirror it and thus win its favor back. This led to his new approach, the latest example being the man on the sidewalk, shuddering as he released his final breath.

Gripping his hands together, he told the driver to go. He would love to be out of the limo during these adventures, but it could get too conspicuous that the same man in a wheelchair was at the scene of several freak accidents. As difficult as it was, he would have to make the sacrifice and play it safe.

Sighing contentedly to himself, he settled back into his seat as the car drove away from the screams and sirens, already late for his next stop.

"Are you certain you wish to do this, Mr. Hobbes?"

Lawrence cut his eyes at the man, a bald and bespeckled older man who had been his dentist for more than a decade.

Lawrence smiled at him, trying to not let any of the animosity he felt show. "Afraid you're not up to the task?"

Now it was the dentist's turn to smile. "No, no. The dental surgeon will take care of everything. I'm just concerned about....well, the nature of the surgery itself. You already have dentures from the accident, so...?"

"This is just something I want, doctor. It doesn't have to make sense to you as long as it's done."

"Of course, of course. You're the boss. I was just curious."

Lawrence grinned toothily, his eyes unpleasant. "It killed the cat, you know. Now finish the examination."

Lindsay Dohan clasped her binder to her chest, protecting it as best she could against the rain as she hopped onto the sidewalk from the bottom step of the school bus. The weight of the homework in her book bag nearly pitched her forward onto her face, but she conquered the inertia at the last moment, taking a couple of stuttering steps forward before ducking her head and pushing against the wind towards her front door.

She had only been in the fifth grade for a month, but she already hated it. She had liked all of her elementary teachers, and had been one of their favorites as well. But this year she was switching classes, which meant six different teachers. Aside from the massive jump in the amount and complexity of homework (most of her teachers suffered under the delusion that they were the only class she had), she didn't like the instability of her new schedule. She liked the comfortable regimen that came from having the same classroom all day. The same teacher, the same students, the same rhythm.

Lindsay dug her key out and got inside hurriedly, her thoughts of school scattering like fall leaves when she heard the radio playing. A cool, light feeling of worry brushed across her brow, casual in its appearance. Her father was home. She had forgotten this was his day off from the bank.

Patrick Dohan had not been a bad father, and she felt that overall he had been very nice to her. But she was deathly afraid of him, nonetheless. He carried a haunted, harried look most of the time, and when he didn't, it was usually replaced by his sudden bursts of anger and yelling.

Nine years before Lindsay was born, her father and mother were newlyweds. They had eloped three months before, and though they didn't know it at the time, Lindsay's mother was already pregnant with her brother, Jacob. While Lindsay's grandparents had not been happy with their teenaged children suddenly running off and getting married, they had accepted it quickly enough--or at least learned to tolerate it.

And they had been willing to help as well. Patrick's father-in-law had offered him a job in the family furniture business, running shipments all over North Carolina and Virginia, with occasional trips further afield. The work wasn't glamorous or anywhere near the top, but it was a small business, and there was time for Patrick to climb. The driving kept him away from home for long stretches of time, but he got long breaks in-between jobs as well, giving him a chance to catch up with his fledgling family.

Then they had gotten a large order from an electronics company in western Kansas, the biggest order of the year. The call had come only due to the fact that the founder and president of the electronics company was an old friend and fraternity brother of Patrick's father-in-law. But the call had come and the order made, and it could all just barely fit in their big load tractor trailer.

Patrick had been working for the company for over a year at this point, and had just completed his certification for big rigs two weeks prior. This was his first haul in the semi, and promises had been made that the office furniture ordered would arrive promptly.

It was more a question of stamina that anything. Plenty of truck drivers have driven longer and harder without becoming dangerous or falling asleep. But this was Patrick's first time, and the road was long and dull. Later, he would swear that he had only been asleep for a moment, and that it wasn't his fault.

Whatever the truth of the matter, he still ran over a man, permanently crippling him. That man was the son of one of the richest men in the Midwest, and when his family sued his father-in-law's business out of existence, it was for no reason other than retribution.

In the years that followed, Lindsay's parents became more and more estranged from her mother's family. They had moved to Georgia when she was three, and soon after, Patrick had gotten a job as a security guard at a local bank. He hated the job, and she sometimes thought he hated his life as well.

He was always so worried, so angry. And there were times she would see him looking at her when he thought she didn't notice. That look bothered her, scared her. She didn't know what it all meant, but she knew she didn't trust her father entirely.

Walking softly, she crept past the living room where he lay listening to the radio, the latest of several beers no doubt perched upon his stomach. She eased down the carpeted hallway, easing her door open and closed again quietly, breathing a sigh of relief when she did not hear him respond to the noise.

Lindsay loved her father very much, and she knew he was a good man. But still, she worried about him. She sat down on her bed, shrugging off her book bag and taking out the first of several books she had to bring home for the evening. She would just stay in here and work quietly on her homework. At least until her mother got home.

Chapter Three

Eric had never had another seizure, though there was a time nearly four years after the first when he thought otherwise. His mother was taking him back home from a trip to the dentist, the station wagon's uneven purr punctuated by the occasional unpromising ping, and he was wholly unaware of his surroundings at the moment. Since he had first learned to read he had done so voraciously, spending hours at a time cooped up in one room or another, pouring over books with a devotion that bordered on desperation.

He was currently in a heavy frontiersman phase, which meant that he was learning all kinds of interesting ways to catch rabbits with a few sticks and bits of string, not to mention the value of keeping your rations stocked and always having an extra firing pin.

He loved the adventure of those books, the icy woods and windswept plains that were so often the backdrop for the noble pioneer or hunter and which inevitably housed all manner of danger, both natural and man-made. But beyond the wild drama of these stories, he liked the underlying themes even better. He enjoyed the solitude and the self-reliance of the main characters, though he would never have thought to express it in that way. The idea that you could be smart enough and brave enough to overcome and even thrive in a hostile and alien environment was very cool.

So it was that he was mere sentences away from finding out if the mountain lion attacked or was scared off by Trapper Bill's cunning ploy when he felt a pressure begin to build in his head unlike anything he had ever felt. He trembled slightly as the book slipped to his lap, his eyes glazing for a moment as the feeling continued to grow. He considered mentioning it to his mother, but she was always so worried about him since his earlier seizure. He hated to alarm her if it was unnecessary, and he thought maybe he was just getting carsick.

Staring ahead, he was dimly aware of the nondescript gray van that passed by even as the pressure in his head reached the bursting point and began to fade. In the moment before the vehicle passed beyond the corner of his eye, he felt certain he had seen a flash of silver light which twisted and roiled along the sides of the vehicle. Then he blinked and it was gone.

When he looked back in the sideview mirror, the van was already growing distant. Within a few more seconds the strange sensation he had experienced had become nothing more than a memory.

He rubbed his eyes and glanced at his mother as she drove. There was a slightly tense cast to her body, a nervous squint in her eyes, an anxious undercurrent to her soft humming in tune with the radio. She hated having to drive in the city, even in the more subdued surroundings they traveled through now. He smiled at her before settling back in his seat, closing his eyes before he realized it.

He awoke at the sound of the turn signal ticking, the gentle swaying of the car as it turned into the bank parking lot rocking his eyes open as he looked around with mild confusion. It was mid-afternoon now, and as he glanced at the car's clock he felt a surge of satisfaction that he was well beyond any threat of having to finish out the day at school.

"Can we have stew for supper?"

His mother glanced over him with a raised eyebrow and snickered. "Stew. You're so weird. Aren't you supposed to crave pizza and hamburgers all the time? You *are* a teenager aren't you?"

Eric laughed and shook his head. "Nope, I'm a little old man. And I like stew."

"Pizza."

"Stew."

"You're thirteen. You want pizza."

"I'm sixty-four. I want stew. Got to get me some stew."

"Sixty-four isn't even that old. Not to me anyway. "

Eric grinned. "Well, you're pretty old yourself, really."

"You're funny. You're getting moldy stew for supper."

As they talked, his mother had entered and slowly slid forward in the drive-thru line at the bank's teller window, which was only two cars away at this point. Eric was about to respond when he noticed three men running out of the bank's side door even as police sirens approached. The men wore black ski-masks and two of them toted duffle bags while the third carried an assault rifle. The robbers cut across the drive-thru lines even as a security guard came through the same side door, his face bloody and his pistol out.

One of the masked men shouted a warning, but it was too late. The slowest of the men was shot in the head, tumbling to the ground with a snub-nosed revolver still gripped in his free hand. Eric watched in fascination as the man convulsed upon the ground even as he heard a string of rifle reports as Assault Rifle sprayed the security guard, killing him. Then his view was obscured as his mother tugged him down underneath the dashboard with her.

"Stay down, honey. This...this will all be over soon."

Eric wondered later what he might have seen if he had been able to watch what happened next instead of just hear. Would he have seen the change that came over the third robber even as Assault Rifle yelled for him to "Get the fuck moving"?

He would hear later that the third man had simply stopped and dropped the duffle bag he carried, turning like a needle in a compass towards the car where Eric and his mother lay crouched and sweating. Assault Rifle had yelled again before snatching up the duffle bags from this man as well as the other who still jerked upon the hot asphalt of the bank parking lot. Rifle then ran away towards ten minutes more freedom before being caught in a getaway car with a dead battery.

But this third man, he was acting quite strangely. He slowly walked towards the car, his movements uneven and stiff as he passed by two cars to get back to Eric's. Eric heard his mother scream as the man peered in with dark, expressionless eyes. The man pulled off his mask to reveal a hard if youthful face and a mouth that hung away slackly from brown teeth. Eric wondered if the man had had a stroke or something, but then the man began to laugh.

"It's you, it's you, it's you, it's YOU!" The words came out in a torrent, the last one ending in a high-pitched squeal as the man brought up a .45 pistol to the glass, pressing it tightly there as he aimed for Eric's head.

It all happened in a moment. His mother screamed again, reaching for him, trying to protect him. A gunshot echoed across the parking lot, and Eric's would-be assassin fell out of view. His screams continued for two heartbeats before a second gunshot silenced him.

Eric knew what had happened. The man who had been shot first was still convulsing, and it had caused him to fire off a shot which hit his partner in the ankle. Moments after the partner had fallen to the ground, the dying man had fired off a second spasmodic shot, striking Eric's would-be murderer in the back of the neck, exploding the other man's throat. He died instantly, with his killer following a few jerky seconds later.

All of that was ridiculous, of course. That chain of events would require so many coincidences it was silly to even think it. Yet Eric knew that was what happened, and so it was.

Police cars arrived seconds later, and the officers at the scene were still shaking their heads and giving Eric and his mother strange looks as they were finally released to go home.

His mother kept having spats of crying as they drove, and as soon as they got into the house she ran to the bathroom. Eric talked to her as she washed her face, trying to say something that would comfort her and make her less afraid. He knew his father would know what to say when he got home, but he couldn't stand to see his mother this way.

Such was his concern for her that he never stopped to dwell upon his own reactions to what had happened. He had been afraid while it was happening, but it had been more of a vague shadow of emotion rather than the thing itself, a place marker for where the dark dread and terror should have been. That in itself should have scared him, but he tried to not think about it.

That night, after his parents had put him to bed for the night, he stared up at the ceiling, replaying the events of the day in his mind, sensing there was more to be understood from what had happened than he could grasp. Closing his eyes, he prayed, thanking God for saving his mother and himself. Praying for the souls of the men that had been killed and the man who had been caught by police. Praying for understanding.

He needed to understand what had happened, because it didn't feel like a miracle. It felt unnatural. He needed to understand what was happening to him. And he needed to understand why he wasn't afraid.

Tertiary: Silencer

The van rocked and squealed on worn out shocks as it moved through the city streets, its interior smelling of metal and stale sweat. Unseen by anyone, Calvin Kurtz licked his lips again, dry and cracked to the point of freely bleeding, and stared straight ahead with a look that was blank but far from glazed over. Occasionally the radio bolted under the dash between the two up front chirped or squawked, but he did not acknowledge it. He had in fact not given any response whatsoever to anything in the outside world for the last three months.

The van was stark and gray, wholly unmarked by any state motto or institutional insignia. The interior of the van was much the same, its design being wholly based upon utility and perhaps paranoia. The front of the van was the same as any prison transport van, though it wasn't one. Behind the front seats was a divider made of heavy steel wire sandwiched between two sheets of Plexiglas. The rest of van was devoted to one chair, bolted to the floor in the center of the cargo area. Made of metal and high-resistance plastic, the chair contained numerous braces to restrain the occupant, and all were employed upon Calvin at the moment. He sat there silently, however, apparently quite complacent if not comfortable on his throne. His breath was faint and shallow, barely stirring the black cloth of the hood that covered his head.

They had been driving for over two hours, but they did not have much longer before reaching their destination. The drivers were nervous and more than a little afraid, and not without some reason. Anyone who deserved the level of security this man had received deserved some consideration, and if the rumors about Calvin Kurtz were true, there was more to the man than a catatonic who had murdered his wife three months ago.

Raziel trailed along behind his charge, staying much closer than was required by his sight. He had always taken his work seriously, always knowing the honor and responsibility of doing the work of the High, but there was more to his diligence now. Something far more personal.

Four years now, four years since his desire to watch over this child had become more than a Holy charge. Four years ago, this child had seen him when he had not wished to be seen. The child had seen him and spoken words that he had known were meant for him and him alone.

So now he followed him, pursuing him as relentlessly as a greyhound would a rabbit, protecting him if it was deemed appropriate. But still, he wondered. The child's existence was a mystery to him. Eric's purpose in the High's plan was wholly unknown to him and to those few he had asked about it. But that was to be expected, and by itself was not at all troubling. But the child had seen him. Had spoken to him.

He was beginning to resent this child.

These thoughts were wiped from his mind as he looked away from the car that Eric Talbot rode in, on his way home from a dentist's appointment. He tensed, phasing several levels closer to Eric's reality as he saw the gray van approaching in the opposite lane.

He could not tell for certain what was contained within, but it was powerful. A cold and silvery light danced and writhed in and out of the van, shifting between levels as it undulated on some unknown tide or breeze. He felt a tension building as the two cars grew closer, a background hum that was ominous in its inscrutability. He shifted down to one level away from Eric and the van, waiting as the tension grew. Then it was gone. The van and car had passed, and Raziel found himself wondering what had just occurred, or almost occurred. He followed along behind Eric for several seconds before pausing again.

The thing in the van, whatever it was, could be a grave threat. It should be investigated.

But not by him. He had his charge.

And yet he wanted to know. He deserved to know. It wasn't disobeying, but simply being proactive. And who better to learn of this unknown danger than the boy's own protector? There really wasn't any choice at all.

And with that, he turned his back to the child and followed after the van and whatever it might contain.

Calvin Kurtz whispered to himself, softly at first. The sound was far too low to be heard by his keepers, and if it were overheard, it would make little difference. It was word salad and nothing more, a mix of fevered phrases that would have no significance to the casual listener. Noteworthy, given the fact that it was the first noise outside of occasional flatulence that had issued from Calvin in quite some time, but ultimately worthless.

"Train...Blueberries...In the cave...the CAVE...blue...blueberries...knock knock...surprise...."

Calvin chuckled softly to himself, and that did get the guard in the shotgun seat's attention.

"What the...you finally wakin' up?"

The driver frowned at his partner and shook his head sharply. "No conversation, no contact. Remember? No matter what he does."

Shotgun nodded, looking slightly surly as he turned back to the front and settled back into his seat. Watching aimlessly as they passed another car, he missed Calvin's seizure.

The seizure was eerily silent, with only the webbed fabric of the chair's restraints making a faint creaking noise. Curtis himself made no sound at all as the cords stood out in his neck and he slowly jerked in his seat, electrocution in slow motion.

Curtis tasted the faint copper of his blood where he bit his tongue, but paid it no mind. His eyes were tracking the car he could not see, marking the thing that has passed so close to him. His expression was a mixture of awe and some other, more complex emotion as he leaned out against the restraints as far as he could. Eventually he relaxed, easing back into his normal posture of catatonia, the only sign of what had transpired the sweat cooling upon his forehead and lip as his breath grew shallow once more.

"It was the damnedest thing, doctor. It's a miracle that we have this tape at all."

Raziel watched as the clinician looked at the federal agent with a mixture of boredom and irritation. Clearly not really caring, the doctor asked his next question in some halfhearted attempt to satisfy the agent's apparent urge to tell the story.

"How *did* you get the tape, Agent Murphy?"

"It was part of the Kurtz' security system. He had money up the ass, as you know. Well, they had cameras that came on when they set the alarm to away or night-time mode. They had both gone to bed already that night, so the alarm was on night mode already. Then she wakes up around 2:35 am and finds him out of bed. She goes to find him, which leads her to the living room, where he's just sitting staring into space. We don't have it on this copy of the tape, but on the full version, he had been sitting there without moving or doing anything for fifty-three minutes before she came in. No indication of anything odd before that."

The doctor looks slightly more interested, but only slightly. "I see. What happened next?"

With a smile and flourish worthy of any carnival barker, the agent pushed the tape into the machine. "Then this happened."

Raziel watched the grainy monochrome footage, starting with Kurtz alone in a chair, staring vacantly. Then a woman enters, her posture showing signs of concern. She says something, but her face is turned away from the camera, so there is no hope of finding what it might have been. At first, there is no response from Calvin Kurtz, and she draws closer a few steps, curiously cautious in her gait.

Then Kurtz looks up at his wife, and speaks briefly. The doctor pauses the film.

"What's he saying there? Do you know?"

"We had the tape analyzed, and our lip readers tell us that he was saying 'This is what you were born for.'"

The doctor frowned and pushed play.

Kurtz' wife is still fifteen to twenty feet away from him and she is visibly affected by his words. He has stopped looking at his wife again, and does not look at her as she begins to rise off the floor. She claws at her throat and thrashes as her feet float up and up, her movements jerky and harsh on the poor video. She rotates slowly like a wind chime, her face dark with fear as she twirls lazily towards the camera. Then her hands go from her throat to her chest as a new panic sets in. She rakes at her chest frantically for several seconds before her entire torso explodes, large chunks of bone and meat flying off in every direction. What is left of her body gently lowers to the ground again, a ruined marionette laid down gently as if by a thoughtful child.

The doctor swallows thickly and shuts off the monitor, sitting silently until Agent Murphy speaks.

"So, Doctor. What the fuck happened there?"

Raziel had no breath in his body. He had no lungs to stir or heart to beat—had no organs at all, truth be told. While he had needed to mimic human breathing from time to time when he was visible to living beings, he had no real sense of the sensation of air filling him with life or being driven from his body. But he *was* well-read. And from his readings, he did have some concept of what these things might feel like.

As he turned away from the black monitor, he fought against the weight that pressed against his chest, a strange mixture of anger and dread building that was as alien within him as warm air would be. He clenched his teeth and ascended several levels, feeling his connection to the High grow stronger as he rose, soothing his troubled heart and mind, if only a little. He knew intellectually that he was no closer or farther away from the High, regardless of where or when he went, that his feeling of approach was an illusion formed from his own limitations and wishful thinking. But nonetheless, it was a balm for his fear.

Yes, he had named it now. He was afraid. Not by what he had seen so much as by what it represented. The man on the tape, if such a description applied at all, was an abomination--a cancer on Creation. Raziel had seen all manner of evil in his millenias of service, both human-born and supernatural. Yet the source of this was something else entirely. Something wholly new and damningly familiar.

Watching the video, he had searched out those levels captured on the video tape, seeing lines of force and tendrils of power that stretched out from the man in the chair to that which had been his wife. Stretching to him from something distant and unseen and beyond his kin. But unquestionably evil. If the actions it spawned had not been proof enough of that, its very essence, dark and corrupt, was further evidence.

But why? Beyond the enigma of where this evil came from, what purpose did it serve? He floated one step away from darkness, pondering these things with a troubled heart until he realized the phone was ringing.

Moving down several levels, he listened as the doctor answered it, hearing both sides of the conversation.

"Hello? Doctor Metzinger? We've lost contact with the Center! It happened a few minutes after the new patient was brought in. What should..."

"What do you mean, 'lost contact'? You can't get ahold of anyone?"

"No...no, we can't. What..."

Raziel turned away again, having heard enough. He pulled the location of the Center from the doctor's mind, and moments later he was streaking towards it, certain that he was too late to help. Expecting to find blood and death.

His expectations were fulfilled. He could feel the death coming off of the building like a stench before he reached it, and when he landed within he was stunned. It had been a slaughter. Everywhere was red, covered in blood that was already beginning to thicken. As he walked down corridors, peering into rooms, he saw no signs of struggle beyond the weak thrashings of the victims before they were dismembered.

Partial limbs and bits of meat and wet bone littered the floors like autumn leaves, often in knee-high piles in the high traffic areas. It's as if every single person in the building had been ripped apart simultaneously. Raziel had every idea that was exactly what had happened.

A roar escaped his throat as he raced down several stories to the cells buried at the deep heart of this place. There was no need to check for the wounded, for survivors of any kind. There was only one living thing left in this building. For the moment.

Raziel ripped the metal door off of the padded cell which contained Calvin Kurtz, tossing it aside as he ducked into the small, dimly-lit room. The man looked up at him as he became visible, a smirk on his face. In this light, the balding, middle-aged man looked as if he was already dead.

"Like my handiwork, Guardian?"

"Monster!"

"Well....yes. But that's kind of the point."

Raziel took a threatening step forward. "Point? There can be no point to the wholesale slaughter of innocents."

Calvin rolled his eyes. "You really are an imbecile, Guardian. Pathetic. Perhaps I should just kill you, as well."

Raziel smiled savagely, flexing his hands. "You cannot kill me, filth. The same cannot be said for you, however."

Suddenly he felt a strange tug at the center of his being, a sense of unease that almost broke the surface before being lost in the dark depths of his anger and indignation.

Calvin licked his finger, which Raziel noticed for the first time was bleeding badly. "Are you threatening me? I'm very frightened."

"You are unnatural. You are a murderer."

"You're very boring."

Raziel surged forward gripping Calvin by the throat and lifting him several feet up in the air. "What *are* you, monster? Tell me!"

Calvin laughed with what little breath he had left. "That's what galls you, isn't it? That you don't know. That you can't know. That your Master doesn't deem you *worthy* to know or do anything but chase around a little boy like a fucking dog."

The room began to shake as Calvin laughed again, his eyes rolling wildly in his head. The walls began to buckle as he screamed. "I will kill again, and again, and again, and again, and you can't stop me, Dog." He glared at Raziel as he said this, looking down on him. Mocking him.

Raziel rammed his fingers into Calvin's eye sockets, fracturing the front of his skull even as he snapped the man's neck. He was suddenly weak, stumbling and then falling to the ground, dropping Calvin's corpse. A surge of panic rushed through him only to be replaced by chilling dread as he realized what had happened. He could no longer feel the High's presence. Moving up and down several levels, he still felt nothing. He screamed in agony and beat his hand upon the padded floor of the cell, suddenly noticing the words written there for the first time, red with Calvin's own blood:

I WONDER WHAT'S HAPPENING TO ERIC RIGHT NOW?

Then he understood, and the next moment he was streaking back to Eric, relieved to find that he still was able to locate the boy. But when he stopped, he realized where he was. The road he had seen the van on. He had returned to the point where he had turned from Eric to follow the van. The place where his connection to his charge had first been severed.

He felt new dread and fear bloom in his chest like a dark flower as he raced along the routes he suspected they would take, ultimately giving up and heading for Eric's home. He was there when they arrived, looking on as the boy comforted his mother. Raziel tried to pray, and found he couldn't. He tried to return Home, and found he could not remember the way. Finally, he left.

Sobbing softly to himself as he walked, he barely heard his voice being called. When it registered, he whirled around in surprise, feeling a moment's hope that this was his chance at atonement and redemption. When he looked upon the man before him, however, he knew it was not.

This thing was not truly a man. It walked and talk as one, but that was just a shell. His first instinct was to attack, a dog smelling something dark and not right. That's all he was, really. A dog that was being punished.

He did not attack however, because he was angry and afraid. Angry for being rejected by that which he loved more than anything for doing what he thought was best. Afraid at not having his Father's protection any longer. His second instinct was to run away, and he almost did just that. But then the man-thing smiled at him, tipping his hat in greeting.

Raziel went cold as he realized what had happened. The damned boy had been right all along. He had Fallen.

Tertiary: Degree

Ralph Tuggle questioned everything these days. Someone once said something about the unexamined life, and he couldn't recall who said it, or exactly how it was put, but he appreciated the sentiment all the same. His life was well-examined these days.

It would be impossible for him to pinpoint when it started, if it truly has a beginning. If what he suspected was true, perhaps the beast simply took shallower breaths in his youth, his early years of adulthood. Perhaps it was only now that he could hear a whispered intake of air and the stale release of raw meat stench and frantic heat. But perhaps it has been there all along. Perhaps.

It also didn't matter. He held little hope that he could find any solution by tracing the origins. In truth, he wondered if he could find any solution at all. But if not a solution, Ralph Tuggle would at least like an answer to the question that now burned in him constantly.

Was he becoming insane?

Becoming insane, as opposed to going insane. Ralph had never been a literary man, preferring science and formulae to a well-turned phrase. But he had given the matter a great deal of thought, and he certainly did not feel he was taking a trip to insanity--a dream or nightmare land from which he would never return. Instead, he felt that if he was doing anything, he was becoming something else, be it more or less. That he was becoming a force of insanity, a creature of delusion and twisted desires.

But that was getting ahead of things.

Ralph Tuggle was a chemical engineer at PharmLin Pharmacuticals, where he had diligently worked himself up to a management position over the course of the last eleven years. Given the way the economy was going, Tuggle felt he was doing pretty well for himself.

If there was anything that he could point to as being wrong with his life, it would be that he got a bit lonely at times. He'd never married, though at forty-three, he still had plenty of time for that, and it wasn't like he never dated, though not very often, but still, he was very busy, and... Loneliness, yes. But he had a few good friends. He went out occasionally, if often alone. He belonged to a church, though he didn't interact much when he went. Perhaps just a bit of loneliness, but who wasn't lonely?

And he was a good man. He'd never broken the law, he was kind to others--the perfect gentleman. A model employee and a good friend. What more could he ask from himself?

But still.

He first started to consider the proposition that he was insane when he realized how bad his memory was. He had always had a remarkable memory for facts and figures, but his own past had grown more and more where it swam and shimmered before him like a vast mirage, with things darting in and out of focus with no true indication of whether or not they were real.

Examples are always helpful. The first example he could give would be trying to remember if he had ever been to Australia. He was talking with a guy at work about the man's time in the former prison colony when he began internally pondering if he had ever been. After several seconds of inner debate, he determined that he had not.

That was only the beginning of numerous fluctuations and inconsistencies in his memory. Everything from the easily explained (had he run into his boss at the grocery store last month?) to the unquestionably troubling (did he have a sister that died as a baby?). On both counts, he learned through circuitous questions that he had not.

But these were not the only signs of what loomed before him. He found himself moving through stores and other public places with feelings that had previously been alien to him, or so he believed. At first it was just isolation. A sense of being so far removed from those around him that it brought a sense of unreality, as though he was watching a movie or a television show, and he could not truly connect with that which transpired. Over time this feeling grew and changed, peppered more and more with flashes of violent impulse. Wondering what it would be like to attack the person walking by, pondering how he could do it without being caught.

He passed all of this off as normal--or if not normal, at least not *ab*normal--for as long as he could. But when the blackouts began, that became an impossibility. At first, he thought he was just tired and that time was simply going by quickly. But eventually he realized that it was more than that. Much more.

He woke up one night, and on the way to the bathroom he stumbled over his shoes, and in his sleepy haze he barely registered that his loafers had been wet as they brushed his bare foot. When he returned, however, he had woken up enough to check and find that they were indeed wet and strewn with grass clippings. It was raining outside, but it had not started before he had went to bed.

Two weeks later, he found a bus ticket stub mixed in with his spare change. It was to a stop he had never used before and actually had not known existed. At this point, he was almost excited by the mystery of it all, feeling that he was trapped in some old Hitchcock movie starring Ray Miland or perhaps Gregory Peck. He actually took off work one afternoon and went to the bus stop, but he didn't recognize anything there. Ralph had actually planned on tracking down the bus driver that would have been driving and asking the man if he remembered seeing him. But that was before this morning.

He scrubbed his hand across his face, careful to use his left hand as he worried his stubble distractedly. He sat slumped in a kitchen chair, in the same position for the last forty minutes. He was already late for work. His eyes skittered around the room, lighting like a nervous bird upon the gun that lay before him on the table before flitting away again. Back to the gun, then to his right hand, now flaking the blood that covered his fingers.

He was not the best housekeeper, and had planned on wearing the same pants to work today as he had worn the day before. He had pulled them on and was checking his pockets for change when he felt something strange and slightly sticky in his right pocket. He pulled out three teeth, a light coating of jellied blood on them. The blind shock of this was great enough that he didn't panic at first. His brain began trying to rationalize immediately. Then he saw that there were several long blond hairs stuck to one of the teeth.

Ralph shifted in his chair now, feeling a flicker of annoyance that it was not more comfortable and then realizing how absurd the thought was.

He'd weighed his options. He couldn't go to the police or a psychologist. Prison or an asylum would just be a slow death instead of a quick one. He could not do that. Picking up the gun, he looked at it with a sense of wonder at how such a dull looking object, a bit of metal, could have such an effect upon things.

Suicide was wrong as far as Ralph is concerned. But if what he suspected was true, he would have far more to atone for if he let himself live and could not control his actions. Could he really take the risk?

Ralph eased the gun into his mouth, having to spread wide and lock his jaw in an uncomfortable position to accommodate the gun's barrel. The cold metal pinned his dry tongue to the bottom of his mouth, his breath coming in a hurried wheeze from around the edges of his lips. He could end it all now, if he could just be brave for a moment.

Closing his eyes, Ralph made his choice.

Chapter Four

The pulsating buzz of the florescent light overhead echoed in his skull, keeping time with the thrum of his headache. Eric's head had started hurting soon after he had arrived in the hospital waiting room, and it had only grown worse in the four hours since. He watched his grandfather and father talking quietly a few seats away, the drone of their voices comforting but doing little to truly soothe him. The two men were extremely similar, with his father appearing to simply be the younger version of his grandfather, stepped out of the past.

Eric paid slightly more attention to their conversation for a moment, and it became clear that they were just talking about various people they both knew, stories from the past. That is all they really shared, truthfully. The past, and their bonds of blood. They did not have any shared interests that Eric knew of, and they rarely did anything together or talked outside of family gatherings. Much like his relationship with his own father.

The thought of living without his mother terrified him. Aside from the fear of that kind of pain and loss--the pain of losing the person he loved the most in the world--there was the fear of what his life may become if he was left alone with his father. They had never had any major disagreements, even though at seventeen Eric was supposed to be at the apex of his rebellious stage. But just in the two weeks that his mother had been sick, he had felt the cold of isolation creeping into his home life. If it was just him and his father, he would be alone. It was a selfish thought, but at least it was something to think about besides the slow ticking of the clock. The surgery should have been over nearly forty minutes ago.

Sighing, he picked up one of the out-of-date magazines that littered the waiting room. It was a bass fishing magazine that he had already looked at twice, and he had no interest whatsoever in bass fishing, but he still found himself combing back through it for articles he may have overlooked before.

When he started hearing the music, he didn't register it. He kept on half-reading the magazine as the metallic tune unspooled in his brain, slowly spilling across his consciousness until it had to be acknowledged. He looked up and peered around for the source of the music, already knowing that it had to be coming from somewhere beyond the waiting room. He looked over at his father and grandfather, but they were still talking, having paid the new sounds no mind. He muttered something about going to the vending machines and stood up.

His father turned to look at him for a moment, his eyes weak and skittery. "Don't go too far." Eric knew that his father lived and breathed for his wife, and if she didn't make it his life would effectively be over. He felt pain grip his stomach at the thought of his father condemned to living the next forty years alone and pining for his mother, and he resented his father's weakness. Resented the pain that his father's love would cause.

He pushed the thought away and focused on finding the music again. The sound of it was fuller when he reached the hallway, but still undeniably tinny. Turning in the direction it seemed to come from, he trailed slowly down the hall, glancing into several rooms before seeing a man leaving a room several doors up. The man was well-dressed and looked to be in his late-forties, his sandy brown hair peppered through with streaks of white. Eric looked at his face as they passed, but he found later that he couldn't remember what the man had actually looked like. Giving the man a slight nod, he slowed down as he walked past the room the man had left, realizing as he passed that the music came from within.

He stopped outside the room for several moments, his curiosity warring with his sense of propriety. He knew he should leave well enough alone and just go back to the waiting room. He knew there was nothing here for him, and that it was wrong to intrude upon a stranger's illness, a stranger's pain. Licking his lips, he rocked on his feet and began to move away before turning back and slowly pushing the door open.

The room was draped in cool shadows, the only light given by the low wattage fluorescent light that hung on the wall. The air was sterile and filled with the whisper-hum of the machines keeping the woman in the hospital bed alive. She was an old woman, in her eighties and clearly near the end of her days. Her arms were all crepe-skin and blue veins, and her eyes moved tirelessly beneath lids thinned and bruised by age and failing health. Eric turned from her to the source of the music that filled the room--it sounded like a waltz of some kind.

Twin shelves of dust and particle board were attached to the far wall of the room; a pair of wilted flower arrangements and some old newspapers lay atop the higher shelf. Upon the lower, finally winding out the last of its music, a small silver music box sat open, a golden key in its side slowing down as the final notes played. He shut the music box on the last sounds and picked it up, turning it over in his hands. It was engraved with various designs, but the lid held the only recognizable image. It was a partridge in a pear tree.

The small and poorly wrought carving hardly warranted such a specific description, but Eric knew that was what it was. It looked just like a silver Christmas ornament his mother had bought for him years ago.

"On the first day of Christmas, my mother gave to me..."

He almost dropped the box at the voice, but managed to slide it clumsily back onto the shelf as he turned around to see that the man he had passed in the hallway had returned. In the cold dim light of the room, the man's smile seemed artificial.

"I'm sorry. I just heard the music and was curious. I..."

"No need to apologize, son. No need at all. Sit down for a bit and visit. I'd like the company after spending so much time in the dark with no one to talk to."

Nodding, his heart still hammering in his chest, Eric sat down on the hard vinyl sofa underneath the shelves while the man sat down in a plastic chair nearby. They sat in silence for several moments, the man looking at the woman in the bed while Eric looked around the room, feeling more awkward by the second.

"Life is funny, you know. Not funny, ha-ha, though it can be that too, of course."

"Um, yeah." Eric shifted uncomfortably on the sofa cushion, wondering how long he should stay before it would be okay to leave.

"People live their lives, simultaneously thinking that they are the center of all of Creation and that they are utterly alone." The man laughed, finally turning to look at Eric, his eyes in shadow. "You do understand the inherent paradox in that, don't you? On the one hand, they think that everything that exists, exists for them. That they are the end all and be all. On the other, they think that nothing they do matters, that the world is at best uncaring and at worst actively hostile towards them and their lives. Do you know why people think these things?"

Eric hesitated, trying to come up with some kind of answer that might satisfy, but ultimately he just gave a slight shrug and shook his head. The man took several deep breaths, the air whistling like the wheezing whispers of the machines around them.

"They think this way because they want to be gods and martyrs. People are a selfish and egotistical breed, and they want to have omnipotence without the guilt or responsibility, martyrdom without the pain or loss."

Swallowing, Eric stood up. "I should get back to my family now. They'll be waiting on me." He didn't even want to comment on what had been said, fearful it would lead to more ranting. The man went on speaking, apparently not noticing or at least not caring that he was leaving.

"People fail to realize that nothing can be gained without sacrifice. Without loss. Without risk. That is the way of things. As natural as physics."

Eric nodded and gave a weak smile. "It was nice talking to you." Then he was out the door, his hands sweating as he made his way down the hallway to the waiting room. The man's words had troubled him more than they should have. The words or the man, something had bothered him a great deal, and when he saw the doctor sitting with his father and grandfather, he knew the news being delivered as though it were the next note in a familiar song.

He stood at a distance until the doctor left, the man not meeting his eyes as he passed. Then Eric approached, his father rising to meet him, his face ashen. "Come on, Eric. Let's go somewhere where we can talk."

The low whirr of the drink machines reminded Eric of the equipment keeping the old woman alive down the hall, his fingertip slowly tracing the whorls in the fake wood covering the tables that crowded the small snack room. His head was buzzing with the white noise of panic and shock, his mind stuttering like the final instant before a deadly crash.

"Eric...She's gone. Jesus God, she's gone." His father's head drooped like a dying flower, his gray and thinning hair shaking slightly as he choked back a sob.

"How did it happen, Daddy?" Disconnected. So far from the pain and fear and loss.

Several seconds went by before his father spoke again, his voice thick. "Her system was already so weak. The doctor said her body just couldn't take the strain of the surgery."

"There wasn't any other choice."

His father looked up, his eyes blazing for a moment. "I know that, damnit." Then the fire left him as quickly as it had come, his face crumpling as he lowered his eyes and whispered. "I know that." The older man fidgeted, his hands washing themselves before fluttering to his face like startled birds. "We should get back." He stood and began to walk out of the room without another word.

"I'm going to stay here for a minute, okay?"

His father paused but didn't turn. "Fine. Don't be too long." With that, he walked out of sight.

The first few moments that Eric realized his mother was dead, he was wrapped in a cocoon of disbelief and shock so complete that he had no real thought or feeling about what had happened. No opinion or concern.

As he sat there, running his fingers over the patterns in the table again, the reality of it began to soak through his protection like icy black water. At first it was a cold presence, foreboding but still distant. Then a tentative touch upon his consciousness, a shiver of realization of what had actually occurred. Then a rush of chilling truth, sinking into his bones and his heart. His mother was dead.

It hit him like an epiphany, followed by a string of thoughts and images as his mind darted between memories of the woman and thoughts of what consequences her absence would bring. These things were both selfish and selfless, stretching across his drowning mind in such a fashion that it was hard to tell where the love ended and the self-preservation began. But underneath it all was pain and anger, both without reason or any real target. But building in him with every moment.

He clenched his hands into fists as he began to cry, softly at first. The tears began to trickle and then stream down his face, his body as rigid as a seizure. He began to wail--a soft, animal sound--and put his head down, his fevered forehead pressed against the cool surface of the table. He felt the pain growing in him, and he finally stopped fighting against it, letting it overtake him.

Eric sat there sobbing for several minutes, his head nestled in the semi-darkness of his arms and his stomach a churning ball of ice. The flashes of thought and memory continued, but he realized that the pain and anger had grown more manageable if not more bearable. He raised his face slowly, his mind still cottony. It took several seconds for him to truly hear the alarms going off all over the floor, and he was already to the door when he heard the first of the screams.

"Lindsay, we've got a walk-in. Can you get him?"

Meredith turned away from the open door of the supply room, walking back out front as if she had already received her reply. Lindsay rolled her eyes and stowed away the remains of her sandwich, brushing crumbs from her pants as she stood from the metal folding chair she had been perched on.

She glanced in the crooked mirror hung over the sink in the cramped and narrow space, brushing her black hair out of her face as she checked to see if she was presentable.

At twenty-two, Lindsay felt she had little going for her aside from her looks, and she was cute at best. She had nice eyes and a pretty mouth, but her nose was too short and her hair too limp for her to be truly beautiful. But as with so much in life, it would have to do.

Sighing, she washed her hands and dried them on a cast-off towel as she put on her apron and her best false smile. She had been working at the hair salon (if you could actually call a place that charged ten bucks for a haircut a salon) for a little over three months now, and she still felt that Meredith was just looking for a reason to get rid of her. That might be paranoid, but only if it wasn't true.

As she approached the front desk, she saw a guy around her age sitting in one of the chairs in the waiting area. He would have been handsome if not for his expression, which floated somewhere between a scowl and a look of deep concentration. He had been staring into space, but he looked up as she approached, his mouth twitching in what might have been a smile as he nodded in greeting.

Running her finger down the sign up sheet, she found his name. "Eric? That you?"

He nodded again and rose. He was a big guy, and his size might have been intimidating if he didn't move with such care, such hesitancy. She looked him over for a second, thinking how odd he seemed, before waving him back. "Come have a seat."

He settled into the chair uncomfortably, keeping his eyes down except for an occasional quick glance up at her in the mirror. He was starting to creep her out, but she pushed it aside.

"So how do you want it?"

He shrugged, which was typical of a lot of guys when asked that question, as if expressing an opinion about what their hair looked like would some how rob them of their manhood. It came as no surprise, but it was still mildly irritating, especially when she was already in a bad mood. "Want me just to shave you bald then?"

The man started slightly in the chair, his eyes startled as he looked up at her, a smile lightening his expression after a moment. "Er...no. I, well...just trim it." His hair was an unruly shock of brown at the moment, and it wouldn't look much better with just a trim, but that wasn't her business. She nodded and started to work.

She didn't actually like cutting hair, and it was far from what she had wanted for herself at this point in her life, but she did enjoy the mindless rhythm of it. She could appreciate the fact that a real stylist would actually put a good deal of concentration into their work, but she worked at a strip mall in Marietta and she was not a good stylist. She was not accomplished at anything.

In truth, the only thing she had ever done that she was even vaguely proud of was getting away from her family. It had taken nearly two years to sever the ties completely, but she had done it. She lived less than thirty miles from her father, but he had no clue where she was, and that was how she wanted it.

"So what do you do for a living?" She hated going through the litany of small-talk, but she had learned over time that it was the only reliable way to get repeat business and sometimes even tips. And guys didn't need much encouragement to talk about themselves.

"I work at Gambino's. The Italian restaurant down the street?"

She nodded and glanced at the clock in the mirror. "It's nearly noon. Shouldn't you be at work for the lunch rush?"

He shrugged, licking his lips nervously. "I'm just the dishwasher and busboy. It'll be a few more minutes before that gets heavy. And I felt like I needed to get my hair cut."

"Yeah, it was getting a bit long. Well, if you wear it short at least...Um, so Gambino's. I've never tried it. Any good?"

The man grimaced slightly and looked up at her. "It's shit. I wouldn't go there if I were you."

Lindsay paused for a moment, again disquieted by him. "Man, you're just a walking advertisement for the joint, aren't you?"

"Just being honest."

She was about to say more when she heard the electric chime signaling the front door being opened. It was one of her few regulars. Every three weeks at noon on Thursday. A nice older man, and a good tipper to boot. Lindsay smiled and gave him a wave before looking back at the guy in her chair. She saw he was looking over at the older man and she turned his head back to the mirror and began cutting again. No need having him creep out one of the only decent customers she had.

She stopped asking questions after that, both because he bothered her and because it would only slow things down and keep the next guy waiting. Within another five minutes she was done and he was at the register, scratching at the loose hairs under his collar while he handed her a crumpled pair of fives.

"Thanks, Eric. Have a good afternoon." She smiled and began turning towards her regular, but suddenly the man grabbed her hand gently. She jumped and turned back to him, eyes wide.

"Be careful, okay? Be careful." His expression hadn't changed, but his eyes seemed more alive, and his voice was full of emotion.

She jerked her hand away and stepped back, unsure what to do or say--what reaction was appropriate or smart. But then the question was moot, as he had walked out of the store without looking back.

Pushing her hair behind her ears, she took a moment to recover before turning to smile at her regular, waving him back even as he stood.

"Come on, Mr. Tuggle. Come on back and have a seat."

Chapter Five

Eric picked at the plate of cold food before him, idly tracing patterns in the congealed sauce while he worried. Worry and guilt were constant companions of his now--ever since the hospital and leaving home. Over a year later, he sat in this restaurant an hour after his shift was over, picking at leftovers from the lunch rush while worrying about himself and the haircut girl.

He had always known things weren't quite right, of course. He was bright enough to figure out that some of the things he saw and felt weren't normal. But the times that it happened were rare. And they had always passed. The strange times frightened him, but they never stayed, and he'd feared that pursuing answers might change that.

His parents had known something of it as well, though they never said it. Not until the night at the hospital. The night he lost his life.

In the months since, what passed for his life had seemed to grow dim, a dull and endless loop of crap jobs and people he never really got to know. He would work a job for awhile, but as soon as he felt himself beginning to get comfortable, to begin to like the people and the place, he would move on. His reason for this was simple, for as his life had paled and thinned, the strangeness that was now ever-present had seemed to solidify and grow stronger.

It began with the flashes. At any given time or place, he might have a burst of...something. Call it intuition, or some kind of mental hiccup. Whatever it was called, it came as natural as thought--only the thoughts were of people he had never met, doing things he had never seen or known. It was almost as if he was remembering some scrap of a story he had read or a movie he had watched, only he knew that wasn't the case. It had a different quality to it. It was as if he were receiving glimpses into other people's lives.

Some were mundane. A man eating breakfast, a boy putting on his pads before a football game. Some were more disturbing. A woman putting on her makeup as she giggled to herself, knowing that her husband was being murdered at his office that very minute.

They came as random flashes of thought at first, alien and bizarre. As time went on, they started to become spiraling daydreams that he found troubling in their detail and length. People he didn't know and lives he had never touched.

At first Eric made excuses, and then he thought he was going insane. He went to a doctor once--a general practitioner instead of a psychologist, as he had still hoped it was a biological problem instead of a mental one at the time. But he feared having his excuses taken away, and so telling himself that it was too much money, he left the waiting room before his name could be called.

As time passed, it became harder to ignore the strangeness that followed him like a shadow. He would meet people and have an overwhelming feeling of misfortunes that would befall them. A cashier at the grocery store near his apartment would have a car accident in the next few days. One of the cooks at Gambino's would go home to find his wife crying over the lump she had discovered that morning. Some days, he would find himself awash in the misery, pain, and fear of strangers. The stink of it lay thick on his clothes and seeped into him through his pores, the taste of it curdling on his tongue and making his gorge rise.

And through it all, through all the worry it caused and all the pity he felt, the thing that scared him the most is that he stopped thinking he was insane. He no longer questioned why it happened, but had accepted it as a natural part of his life. Looking back, Eric could never pinpoint when this transition occurred.

Regardless, he had learned to live with it. His acceptance allowed him to ignore it, and by ignoring it, to never consider what it might mean. Usually, at least.

But three weeks ago he had gone to have his haircut after work. He had walked into the same place he had gone today and felt awash in a sense of foreboding that hung in the air. It wasn't something about the place itself, or anything that was going on at the time. It was more of a warning of something to come. He looked around at the few people in the hair salon and knew that whatever it was, it wasn't about any of them. Eric couldn't have said how he knew that anymore than he could have explained why he turned and left the place without another word.

One of the things that had come from his acceptance of his peculiarities was that he relied on his instincts a lot more, especially when it came to the flashes. If he felt he should do something, he just did it, without questioning why. He had no way of knowing if it helped him or not, but it hadn't seemed to hurt, and he felt the instincts had to serve some purpose, no matter how obscure.

In any case, it was less than an hour before he had put the salon out of his mind, and as his hair grew shaggier, he didn't even consider going back or heading elsewhere to get his haircut. Until today. Then he got the urge to get his haircut again, and he followed the urge back to the salon.

When he entered, Eric felt that same sense of foreboding as before, but much stronger, as if a film covered everything, thick and gray. He gritted his teeth and sat down in the chair, trying to ignore the way being there made his skin crawl.

Then the girl—her name was Lindsay—had walked up and he had two thoughts simultaneously. That she was one of the most beautiful girls he had ever seen and that she would be dead in a matter of hours.

He had sat there, his stomach twisted in knots as he debated what to do. He had wrestled with telling her all while she cut his hair, but what could he say? How could he warn her so he wouldn't sound like a lunatic? He couldn't think of any way to make her believe him.

And what if she did believe him? He didn't know how or why she would be killed. He couldn't tell her anything useful. What if him telling her only made it worse and more people died? So he was left giving her lame advice while he racked his brain for something better.

He had considered just ditching work and watching out for her until the time came. But how certain could he be that he would actually be able to save her? He couldn't stay too close or someone would notice and think he was stalking her. And what if it was a car accident or a brain aneurysm?

Maybe he was just a coward, he thought. So paralyzed by his self-pity and isolation that he was making up excuses for why he shouldn't get involved. But no, he was being honest. He had not known how best to help the girl.

He had stopped on the sidewalk, looking down at his feet as he warred with himself again. Letting out a breath, he had rubbed his eyes and walked on to work. He decided to trust his instincts again--to trust that he would know when and how to help her when the time came.

Now as he sat here picking at his food, he cursed himself for being so stupid. He wasn't going to get any sense of how to help her. He had known it all along on some level. He was just a selfish fucking coward who didn't want to get involved, didn't want to *bother*. It might interfere with him thinking about himself. He could have....

He dropped his fork as the feeling came over him, rushing through the cells of his body like ice water, filling him inch by inch. His hands curled into balls as he stood up, unsteady on his feet. This was something new and it scared him. But he also knew it was what he had been hoping for—a way to help the girl.

He felt a panicked urge to struggle against the impulses washing through him and pushed it down. This was the only way to save her. Swallowing hard, he surrendered to it.

Fifteen minutes later Eric was across the street from a row of apartments. He assumed that one of them belong to the girl, Lindsay, though he wasn't sure. He was lucky that it was so close to where they both worked. While he didn't know, he figured she wasn't home yet. For now, he just had to wait and see what happened next.

There was a small playground on this side of the street, consisting of a see-saw and a pair of swings with plastic netting for seats. Giving a glance around, he decided the swing was the best choice for his stakeout, even if it made him look vaguely like a lurking pedophile. Rocking back and forth, he kept watch on the sidewalk and driveway of the apartments, hoping that she would walk up rather than drive so he would have an easier time spotting her.

He thought about how he had gotten here in the first place. It wasn't like losing control, some kind of possession where he watched as his body jerked along some invisible path to a part of town he had never seen before. He made every movement, but in an absent way, as if going through the motions of a dance as familiar as his own skin.

It was the same way when he stood up and began running across the road, the knowledge blooming in his mind that Lindsay had beaten him there after all, and that at that moment she was opening the door on her killer.

There was no hesitation when he reached the door, no consideration that this was the wrong door or that nothing was happening. He twisted the knob, feeling little surprise that the door was unlocked. Barreling through, he slammed into the back of a man standing just inside the entry hall. The man pitched forward with a surprised 'whuff' sound, landing on his knees. The apartment was dimly lit, with the fading evening light providing little illumination through the partially closed blinds of the only nearby window. Eric's eyes flew around as he caught his footing, his gaze finding the shadowy form of Lindsay, prone and still.

Seeing her that way, his mouth went dry and he moved to help her even as he saw movement out of the corner of his eye. The next moment he was on the ground, the smell of sweat and panic filling his senses as the man atop him struggled to grab his arms, huffing wetly through his mouth.

"She's mine....she's...mine!"

"Get off of me, you crazy fuck." He struggled against the older man, feeling the beginnings of fear seep in around the edges of his adrenaline haze as he realized that he may not be strong enough to fight him off. He managed to punch the man's neck as one of his hands was freed from the lunatic's grasp, his rush of relief and triumph short-lived as he saw the dull red glint of a bloody survival knife back in the other man's hands.

Time slowed as the killer's eyes moved from the knife back to Eric, his confidence returning as he gripped the weapon more firmly in his hand. At the same time, Eric realized that a metal bar stool stood nearby. Stretching out his free hand, he made a quick and fleeting grab for it as the knife began its downward arch towards his chest.

He moved the leg of the stool just enough to overbalance it. The man atop him had leaned forward slightly as he moved the knife down toward his next kill, and in slow motion, the edge of the stool collided with the side of the man's head. Instead of sliding or bouncing off harmlessly, the stool stayed against the side of Ralph

Tuggle's head even as his eyes bugged out with almost comic surprise. Then he slumped to the side, finally pulling the chair free to tumble to the floor.

Eric looked back and forth between the man and the instrument of his salvation, his brain numbed by this touch of the surreal. He pushed himself into a sitting position, getting clear of the killer, still wary it was a trick of some kind. But as he moved nearer to the man, he knew Tuggle wasn't playing possum. It was then that he saw a trickle of blood ebbing out of the man's temple from a small puncture wound. Frowning in confusion, he picked up the stool and immediately saw more blood on its surface. It took only a moment to find the source of the injury.

The bar stool, made of some fairly cheap metal and painted a lime green, had a half-inch metal spur jutting out from its rounded edge. This jagged tooth of metal was now covered in blood, having buried itself in his would-be murderer's temple. He still couldn't begin to fathom how it was possible or to comprehend the odds against it, but for now he had to accept it. He....

He had forgotten all about saving Lindsay. Turning to her, his heart suddenly in his throat, he saw that a dark pool of blood had spread around her, apparently coming from the darker stain on her side. Eric remembered the blood on the knife and felt his stomach clinch. He tried to check her pulse but couldn't find any.

Grabbing her hand--cool and limp, small and fragile—he despaired as he began to squeeze it and say her name. Gently and softly at first, and then harsher and louder.

"Wake up. Wake up! You have to wake up, Lindsay."

Her eyes fluttered and rolled. After a moment she looked at him with confusion. "Why are you here?"

He smiled at her, trying to look reassuring. "I'm trying to help you. Just hang on while I get help. You're hurt."

She grimaced, "Yeah, that bastard stabbed me." She passed out again for a moment before coming back with a weak smile on her face. "I'll hang on. Just....just hurry."

Tertiary: Parlor Trick

Sandra came out from the freezer, sighing as she dumped a package of ground chuck onto the counter to thaw. "It's going to be awhile, Patrick."

He turned away from the grill and tipped her a wink. "I've got enough lard and sawdust to make it through the next hour or so." He studied her while she laughed, his eyes flickering from her face to her body and up again.

"Yeah, yeah." She moved to lean against the table beside him, looking at the clock on the wall. "It's already nearly two. It'll be slow as molasses until school lets out this afternoon."

He nodded. "You're probably right. We'll have to find some way to kill the time."

Sandra laughed again as Patrick grinned at her, heat slowly filling her face as she reminded herself for the hundredth time that he was married. Yes, but how happily? She wondered.

His little jokes aside, he had always been the perfect gentleman. He was such a kind man, but had such a sadness about him. As if he was nobly shouldering some terrible burden. She had worked at the diner for just under a year now, and she had just about decided that she had fallen in love with him.

She knew she was younger than he was, and she suspected she was being more than a little stupid. But that's half the fun of being young, wasn't it? She knew he had to feel the same way. He was just too honorable, too good, to admit it.

She was about to say something else when she heard the bell over the front door tinkle. She rolled her eyes and pushed herself away from the table, returning his earlier wink before heading out to greet the diner's latest customer.

Her spirits lifted slightly when she saw the man wore a sharp white suit. Her first thought was money and the second was that he was likely light in his loafers, but when she attempted to study his face she found herself uncertain. His face was so plain, so...ordinary. She found she had trouble holding it in her mind when she wasn't looking directly at him. So what if he's not a handsome charmer? Didn't mean he wouldn't be a good tipper.

Flashing her best smile, she edged up to the counter as he sat down, sitting his matching white hat on the stool beside him. "Hey there. How're you today?"

The man returned her smile, his eyes twinkling as he spoke. "I'm doing fine, quite fine. I'll just take some coffee for now."

She would've been pissed at the small order, but she was too busy trying to keep her knees from buckling. His voice. *His voice!* It had sent a thrill through her unlike anything she had ever felt. It was like being wrapped in soft, soothing velvet.

She coughed and nodded, turning to get his coffee in a daze. She sloshed some into the saucer as she returned, her hand trembling slightly as she placed it before him. He favored her with another warm smile and then raised his eyebrows slightly. He leaned forward conspiratorially and she found herself tilting toward him like a sunflower, eager to hear his voice again.

"Would you like to see a magic trick? Just a parlor trick, really."

"Sure! Um, sure. Yeah, that'd be great." She beamed at him, wondering how old he must be. He could have been thirty or ninety. She couldn't tell either way, and she was too enraptured at the moment to find that strange.

Nodding, he plucked a silver dollar from thin air, spinning it on the table. It twirled like a dancer, catching the light as it turned. Then he scooped it up again, rolling it across his knuckles. Flipping it in the air, he caught it and then opened his hands with a flourish, showing that it had vanished.

Sandra clapped as she let out a laugh of genuine delight. She thought she heard Patrick clear his throat from somewhere in the kitchen, but she gave it no notice. Before she could praise the trick, the man opened his mouth and spat out the coin into the palm of his hand. His nimble fingers picked it up and handed it to her. She took it without hesitation, her eyes filled with wonder. The coin was dry and cool to the touch.

"That....that was amazing."

He smiled and shrugged, sipping at his coffee. "As I said, just a parlor trick."

She slipped the coin into her pocket and kept her hand upon it for a moment. It felt almost as wonderful as the man's voice. She forced herself to step back and turn away, not wanting to look overeager. When she turned back a few seconds later, she was dismayed when she saw the man walking out the door. She might have gone after him, but she was overcome by a wave of sickness that brought her to her knees.

She managed to stand again, the sickness lessening slightly but still pervading every part of her body. She felt sluggish and cold, nausea rolling through her stomach as she shoved past the kitchen door to find Patrick cutting lettuce, a dark look upon his face. "That fella didn't stay long. Must have been quite entertain..." He stopped as he looked up and saw her. "God, Sandra. What's the matter?"

"I'm sick. I've got to go home."

He nodded, not questioning. "I'll take you home."

She backed up towards the door. "No, no. I'll be fine. You have to stay and mind the diner. I'll call you if I need anything."

He frowned, looking unsure. "I don't know."

"I'll be fine. I'll see you later." Not waiting for a response, she made her way back out to the front and with an effort shuffled outside to her car. She had forgotten her purse in the back of the kitchen, but her keys were in her pocket, and that was all she cared about for the moment. Her skin was beginning to itch all over, and she felt so *sick*. She'd be better once she got home.

Sandra scratched at her skin in the blue light of dusk, beyond caring about the grey-green scaly surface that seemed to be thickening all over her body. She had been hungry earlier, and had devoured everything in the house. She thought she remembered eating some raw meat from the freezer, breaking a tooth along the way. It didn't matter. None of it mattered. All she wanted now was to sleep.

She stumbled naked to a dark corner of the living room, unaware of the stench that came off her in waves, filling her apartment. She made it to the corner, her eyes fluttering closed for the last time as she sank to the floor. Her lids scaled over in minutes, and by dawn she could not be seen at all. All that was left was a large scabrous mound that had attached itself to the corner of the room, pulsing slowly like an obscene heart. What remained of Sandra was consumed quickly, leaving behind only dark remnants of her final dreams and the fading stench of decay.

Chapter Six

Hurrying down the store aisles, Eric found himself wondering for at least the tenth time today whether it would be too cold tonight. As he scanned row after row for leftover customers or ill-prepared burglars, he regretted his pride for a moment, knowing how much it was costing him. He had lost his hovel of an apartment last week when the rent had suddenly jumped, and he wouldn't get paid again until Friday. As it stood, he had less than twelve dollars and that had to buy him food for the next three days.

His eyes passed over all of the shelves of castoff merchandise, old and tired things that no one wanted any longer. They called it an antique mart, but it was a junk store, filled to its roof with things that served no purpose in the world. Looking at all of this depressed him, reminding him of what little point his own life seemed to have.

Still, he had bigger fish to fry at the moment. He could be introspective and angst-ridden later. Finishing at the front of the store, he gave the thumbs-up to Kelvin, the assistant manager. "All clear. I'll see you in the morning." Without waiting for a response, he headed out into the December night air.

He cursed as the chill hit him, his irritation turning to concern as the wind hit and the residual warmth from his hours indoors was swiftly leeched away. Eric almost turned back, almost said something or asked for help, but he fought the urge. He had only worked there a few weeks, and he had no place asking for anything. Even if they gave him help, he couldn't stand being beholden and couldn't afford the ties to those that helped him. He had to travel light.

Pacing his way down the street, he decided to wait before buying anything to eat. He wasn't very hungry, and he might need something hot later tonight a lot more than he did now. It was another twenty minutes before he reached the park, and as he did every evening, he did a quick walkthrough to make sure that everything looked okay before settling into the spot he had called home for the last four nights.

It wasn't a bad spot as far as things went. The park wasn't overly large and was moderately rundown, but it did have a decaying gazebo in one out of the way corner. At one time it had probably been something to see, freshly white lattice woven into columns and a roof, fresh vines and flowers trailing up the sides. Eric could see this in his mind, and he preferred that image to the reality, a warped and peeling thing that leaned to one side and had bits of brown leaves running through it. While it really did little in terms of providing shelter from the elements, it felt less exposed than other places he had found, and it was peaceful.

He was fortunate that there were few homeless people in the area that used the park, and police rarely bothered those that did. While it was still dangerous and he kept out an eye for someone that might try to do him ill, Eric feared the temperature drop more than anything else. The second night out here he had found it hard to wake, his body leaden as he pulled himself up into the sunrise, his brain fogged from the night's frost. And tonight was colder already.

He had considered a shelter, but given some of the stories he had heard, he was afraid that'd be more of a risk than sleeping out here alone. But still, he could ask *somebody* for help, or call his father even.

"Like hell. I'll be fine." Settling down against the side of the gazebo's railing as he muttered, Eric adjusted his jacket and pants until he was satisfied he couldn't make them any warmer, and then he lay his head back, thinking about how he had come to be here.

He had saved that girl's life over three years ago now, leaving her at the hospital as soon as he knew she was going to pull through. He had called and picked up his last paycheck the next day, unwilling to take any chance that he would run into her again.

The next few months had seen him move away from the Atlanta area and on to first Tennessee and then down to central Georgia. He had worked a couple of jobs in Macon before coming north again, each stop less promising and fulfilling than the last. It seemed that his life was growing thinner and more threadbare by the day, to the point that he was only rolling along to breathe a little longer. Only struggling to survive. Only fighting to not freeze to death.

He would have said he was on the run, but he didn't know from what. He knew he didn't trust himself. He didn't trust what he could do or why he could do it. After what happened when his mother died, he couldn't rationalize the strangeness that shrouded him constantly. The flashes and visions, the bits of information he had come to live with, but could never be at ease about or truly accept. And underlying all of that was the indefinable certainty that all of it was only a foreshadowing of something more that had yet to reveal itself.

The last few months, as Eric grew more and more detached from his life, he had felt that sense of impending *something* growing, as though he were simply waiting in the wings off-stage, waiting for the moment when he would step forward and begin his real life, shedding his old one like a bad dream.

He snapped his head up and realized he had been dozing. He needed to sleep, but he wanted to sleep light. If he stayed still too long, he was afraid he wouldn't wake up at all. Closing his eyes again, he tucked his head down into the collar of his jacket and descended back into darkness.

He woke with a jolt, shaking his head groggily as he forced himself to wake up. It was so cold. More than a sensation, it felt like a state of being, the frosty air its own wholly-encompassing reality as it seeped further and further inside. Rubbing his eyes he stood up and walked around the gazebo floor, shaking his arms and legs to warm them and get back feeling. Again he considered going somewhere else, asking someone for help, but then he looked up through the ceiling of rickety lattice and thought fled from him.

The night sky was the deepest of deep blues, lit by the glow of a full moon and the distant fires of thousands of stars. Sinking to the floor, he eased onto his back, taking in the most beautiful sky he had ever seen. It captivated him instantly and entirely, calling to some deeper part of himself that he had never acknowledged before.

The stars shined out to him, dancing and burning as if only for him. But he knew they burned for each other as well, and for every single thing their light would ever touch. They shined and twinkled against the rich swaddling sky that enveloped the world, always giving, never taking. Always fulfilling their role.

Suddenly Eric felt troubled and he wasn't sure why. He felt some sense of panic and shame, and the feeling was so unexpected and intense that he sat up again, frowning as he realized he must still be half asleep. He debated getting up again, but the sky drew him back. Pushing away the sudden feelings, curling up into a ball against the cold, he turned his head so he could look at the sky again.

Watching the sky made everything feel clean and hopeful, full of peace and promise. He felt a trace of the other feelings skitter across his heart, but he ignored it. Instead he watched the winter night, cold and silent and still. He shifted his gaze to look at the moon, and smiled slightly as he watched it hanging there at the center of things, small and white. He slept deeply.

"Wake up, Eric. Wake up."

He sat up suddenly, gasping in breath as if breaking through the surface of a lake after going to its cold, dark bottom. It hurt to breathe, the cold air burning as it went down. In a moment, however, he began to feel the ache in his bones and had to fight from crying out.

It took him a second to clear his head enough to realize that someone had spoken to him. Turning his head as quickly as his pain would allow, he saw that a man was sitting five feet away from him, propped against one of the gazebo's support beams.

The man was very large, even sitting down as he was. With long brown hair and a brown beard streaked with gray, he would have looked like a biker or ex-hippie if not for his bearing and his eyes, which shone with intelligence and authority.

"You shouldn't sleep outside. Much longer and you might have frozen to death." The man smirked slightly and extended his hand, "My name is..."

"*You*. It's you, isn't it? Why did you come back? Why are you here?"

Raziel's jaw flexed as he smiled at Eric, giving a slight nod. He withdrew his hand. "It is. Does that bother you?"

Eric shook his head, too groggy and confused to know exactly how he felt about this or anything else. "What's your name?"

The man's voice took on a more formal tone. "It is Raziel. On the day you were conceived, I was charged with being your guardian angel."

"Guardian ang...Look, just go on, okay, man? I don't want any trouble. I do remember you, but I don't know what the..." A flood of images swirled through his mind and he did cry out now, gripping his head as it threatened to overwhelm him.

Raziel looked on as if he had failed to notice any change in Eric. "Why don't we go get some coffee and talk this over?"

Eric pushed himself backward, his butt scraping along the cold wood floor as he scrabbled along. "Stay back."

"Come on, Eric. If I'm not mistaken, your little episode just now was you realizing more about me and perhaps why I'm here. Remembering me. So where's your trust?"

Keeping eye contact with Raziel, he sat up fully and then stood slowly, gripping the railing as he tested first one leg and then the other. "Why would I trust you? How could I?"

Raziel looked at him for several beats before giving an answer. "Because I can help you understand why you are the way you are. I'll give you all the answers you need."

Chapter Seven

Eric forced himself to eat slowly, the chili burning his lips as it went down, feeling terrible and wonderful at the same time. A deep and sullen cold filled the core of him, stubbornly refusing to leave his bones even after over fifteen minutes inside the heat of the diner he had been taken to. Sipping some water to cool his tongue, he looked over at the man sitting across the table from him. His guardian angel.

In the light, he could see that the man was well if plainly dressed, with a dark overcoat that obscured his clothing except for a thin strip of what appeared to be a tan workshirt. He wore black boots that rose above the cuffs of dark corduroy pants. All of the clothes were clearly well-made, but they all appeared somewhat incongruous to each other. Eric suspected the man had never given much thought to how they looked.

For now, all of his supposed angel's attention was on him. He waited to talk however, allowing Eric to finish eating before he spoke again.

"As I said, my name is Raziel. Did you know that before tonight?" The man's green eyes were weighing him as he asked.

Eric grimaced and shook his head slowly. "Of course not. I'm not psychic. I just remember you. I don't know anything about you." He paused. "Not really."

"Maybe you do and maybe you don't, but either way we have much to discuss, you and I."

"Like you being my guardian angel?"

Raziel nodded. "Like that, yes. I was your guardian angel for some time."

Shifting in his seat, Eric glanced around the diner, which contained half a dozen other people. He knew he should get away from this man, but there was something about him that held a fascination for Eric. He told himself that it wasn't any foolish hope that the man had any real answers for him, but he didn't quite believe that. Whatever the case, for the moment he stayed, telling himself he would leave the first chance he got. But he had to wait, so the lunatic wouldn't follow him. Playing along couldn't hurt. And something just said had caught his attention.

"Was? You're not my guardian angel any longer?"

Raziel looked at him for a moment before dropping his eyes. "No, not anymore. I've got a new assignment now. Though it does involve protecting you."

"Protecting me? I didn't know I needed protecting."

"You do. But I'll get to that in a moment. First I need to explain some things. You won't believe any of this at first, and you won't ever understand all of it, but I'll tell you enough to give you a clue, and hopefully make my job easier in the long run."

Raziel looked up as the waitress came to take away Eric's bowl and refill their drinks. The man looked down at his glass, a flicker of anger passing over his face like the shadow of a cloud. "Ordering a drink when you're not thirsty. Purely out of the social need. Only an animal could think of something so insipid and pointless. Anything to connect and forget how alone you all are."

"What're you talking about?"

"I remember observing this habit as I did so many human customs--with mild confusion and stronger disdain. Now after a handful of years I do it without thinking." He paused, taking a sip from his glass. "Which I'm alone now too, aren't I?" The last was punctuated by the man's hard stare at Eric, intense and raw with emotion. Then he was all business again, quick as a lie.

"There are a great many things in existence, both in your reality and in a multitude of others. The breadth of Creation is vast, as you may imagine, but its variety and nature is even greater. Order and chaos are just two more human concepts that have no significance in the big scheme of things, with everything flowing in a symphony of burning movement that is endless and beyond beauty." His voice had grown thick and he paused for a moment. Wiping his eyes before going on, his gaze dared Eric to speak.

"There are many entities and forces in Creation, most of them rising and falling, living and dying and living again. Mutable and yet confined to the parameters of their existence and purpose. There are a few things that are outside of such parameters. One of these is Darkness."

Eric waited a moment, weighing his question before asking it. "Darkness? You mean, the dark? Light and dark?"

Raziel gave him a cold smile. "Eric, this will go faster if you spare me the more obvious questions and let me talk." Without waiting for a response, he went on. "No, not darkness in that sense. The darkness you refer to is a phenomenon of the physical world, a contrast created by the Creator so that you may have the gift of sight. It may serve many purposes and have many properties, but it is no more remarkable than dust motes or the air you breathe.

"What I refer to is a Force. I suppose you might refer to it as a force of nature, such as gravity, though that is somewhat misleading for several reasons. First, the Darkness exists across almost every level of reality. Second, it has a consciousness. It thinks, in other words. And third, it is what you would term evil."

Eric had been listening, feeling a sick fascination even as fear began to build in his chest. Now he suddenly felt a flare of anger consuming that fear. He was tired of this. "So, Raziel, just how fucked up are you?"

The other man's expression didn't change. "Just hear what I have to say."

"Why should I? I'm sick of listening to this metaphysical bullshit. You're fucked in the head, and I already have too much weird shit to deal with without adding you to the mix. So what say I pay for my chili and we call it a day?" He started to stand, but Raziel gripped his arm firmly and pushed it back to the table.

"You'll stay and listen to what I have to tell you. It won't be much longer."

Eric tried to move his arm but found he couldn't. The man's grip was like iron. He considered calling for help, but something told him not to. He didn't trust what Raziel would do if he did. Finally he sank back into his seat and nodded. "Fine. So the Darkness is alive and evil."

"Evil, and in fact, one of the oldest and most powerful sources of evil in Creation."

"Is it the Devil?"

Raziel shook his head. "No, not the Devil. It's actually older than what you call the Devil or any other infernal evil, but any comparison would be pointless." He paused for a moment, frustration evident on his face. "Look, have you ever had a computer?"

Eric nodded, his eyes lifting from their scan of the table for any potential weapons. "Sure. Who hasn't?"

"Well, on a computer, you have programs you can run, right? Games, email, whatever, right?"

"Angels know about email?"

Raizel gave his arm a squeeze, just south of hurting. *Don't piss the psycho off, Eric.* "We know quite a bit of everything. Quit interrupting.

"So you have programs you can use. Things you can see and interact with. But behind that, you have all kinds of programs and code running in the background. The things behind the curtain that really keep everything going. With me?"

Eric nodded, remaining silent this time.

"The Darkness is in the background of reality. It is one of the forces that shape things, primarily through pattern and causality."

"Are you talking about Fate?" The question popped out before he could stop himself, and he waited for the man to attack him, start barking, or something worse, but this time Raziel smiled.

"A fair question. No. There is no Fate. But there are forces outside of this reality that exert their influences for good or ill on its inhabitants. This thing I speak of is one of the chief among those.

"By now, you certainly believe more than ever that I'm totally insane, I have no doubt. But you also probably wonder why I'm telling you all of this, correct?"

Eric nodded slightly. "Focused more on the thinking you're crazy, but yes."

Raziel chuckled. "Good enough. Earlier you said the Darkness is alive. But that isn't accurate. The concept of living, any concept of living, only has validity for beings within some level of reality. As I've already said, the Darkness is *outside* of reality. But it wants to change that."

"How's it going to do that?"

"Isn't it obvious?" Raziel leaned forward, his eyes lighting up. "It's going to do it using you."

Raziel went on to explain that the Darkness had been planning for time out of mind to find some means of crossing over into reality. Doing so would allow it to evolve, slowly gaining power and taking over reality, level by level. Finally it had discovered a way.

The human soul is, among other things, a person's only connection to other levels and to that which lies outside the bounds of Creation. Using that connection, the Darkness could siphon a tiny portion of itself into a human vessel. Over a number of years, enough of its essence could make it across to exert influence over reality from this side and open a passage for the Darkness to manifest fully.

Of course, there were many, both good and evil, who would try to stop this from happening. The only way to insure it would go unprevented would be for all of the Darkness' energy to be released from the person at once. At the person's death.

Raziel grinned at him, his eyes sending a shiver through Eric. "And guess who the person is."

Eric felt his stomach twisting into knots, his brain fuzzy-feeling as he tried to deal with what he was hearing. His fears warred with one another. Was Raziel insane or actually telling him the truth?

"So what does that make me then? A bomb?"

Raziel laugh aloud. "A bomb. Yes, I guess that's a good way to look at it. You're a little meat bomb that's going to bring about the Apocalypse."

"Why would you want that? If you're an angel?"

Raziel stopped laughing, his eyes turning dark as he spoke. "You know that already, Eric. You're the one that told me, remember?"

Eric swallowed. "You...You've Fallen."

"Smart boy."

"So are you going to kill me now?"

"Now? Maybe not so smart. Would I have wasted my time telling you all of this just to kill you? No, my orders are to protect you until it is time for you to die. Apparently there is a specific time and place that is the most conducive to bringing the Darkness over. You're not supposed to die until then."

Eric clenched his teeth, feeling anger stir again. He believed now--to some degree at least. He now remembered enough from seeing Raziel before to know he wasn't human, that no one else could see him that time when he was little. When he had his seizure.

Sitting across from the man now, he clenched his teeth hard. The thought of being manipulated, the vulgarity of what Raziel was suggesting, and the apparent joy with which he contemplated it--it all enraged Eric. It sickened him.

"What if I just kill myself now? Stop this little party from happening? You can't protect me from myself. Not all the time."

Raziel snorted. "It's too late for that. If you die ahead of schedule, it'll still happen. It may be messier or more of a hassle than if we wait--I don't know, I'm not a detail man on this stuff--but I've been assured it will happen either way."

"Like I'd believe you."

Raziel grinned again, his teeth a brilliant white against his dark beard. "Try me, meat bomb. I don't lie."

"So I'm supposed to just get abducted by you, letting you lead me around until the proper time for me to die so this great evil can come kill everybody? Um, yeah."

"Actually, you can choose where we go. For now, I'm just along for the ride to make sure no one gets to you. And you can spend all of that time plotting a way to foil our dastardly plans. You'll fail, of course, but it'll give you something to do."

Eric sat there for several minutes, taking it all in. Considering. As much as he wanted it to all be a lie, he didn't think that it was. It felt like the truth. Finally, without looking at Raziel again, he moved to get out of the booth.

"Fine, let's..." Raziel gripped his arm again, stopping him. When Eric turned to him, the man's expression was dark.

"Two more things before we go, Eric. First, you're not special. You were picked fairly at random, and these little visions and insights you have are nothing more than a cosmic burp--a side effect of having the Darkness inside of you. That's why they've gotten stronger as you've gotten older, because more of the Darkness was crossing over. At the end of the day though, you're nothing but another hairless monkey hiding from the storm."

Eric didn't break the other man's gaze, trying to have no visible reaction to his words. "What's the second thing?"

Raziel's face lit up, his smile as genuine as it was savage. "When you die, I'll be the one to kill you."

Chapter Eight

Eric had thought he wouldn't be able to sleep once they were on the road, Raziel radiating menace as he drove out to the interstate. The car was a late model sedan-- nothing special, but at least it was clean and warm. Compared to what he had been forced to get used to lately, that was the next thing to Heaven. Still, he was far too anxious to enjoy his reprieve from the cold, and certainly too worried to sleep.

He felt angry with himself for being unable to discount this man as a lunatic. All this talk of some great evil force was insane, and so was the man that had now abducted him.

"So where to, Eric? Like I said, we've got quite a bit of time before the big day. In the mean time, we can go wherever. I certainly don't care. Look at it as an extended version of a last meal before your execution." The man's voice was light as he spoke, as if he were discussing them going to a baseball game. He glanced over at Raziel, studying him for a moment. The man's face wasn't handsome, but it was strong. It looked like a face that had laughed and smiled quite a bit in the past, but he wasn't smiling now. He looked weary, in fact. Bone-tired.

"Why are you doing this?"

Raziel turned onto the interstate onramp. "I've Fallen, remember? You should know that better than anyone. Well, we're headed north now, so you pick from there."

"I should know that better than...I don't even know you."

Raziel glanced at him, his eyes hot. "Maybe not, but you know *things*, don't you? You know all kinds of things. For all the good that does anyone." He looked back to the road, his mouth a thin line. "Don't worry though. You'll serve a purpose soon enough."

Eric shifted against the door and looked out the side window as the morning scenery passed by. This man was insane. He had to be. But Eric knew he wasn't.

"Nashville, Tennesee."

"Sure thing."

There were the obvious things, of course. Why pick out some guy sleeping in a gazebo for your fixation? How did he know Eric's name? And beyond all of that, Eric remembered him. And he remembered that no one else had seen the man that had watched over him that day. Maybe all of that could be explained away. Maybe it couldn't. But in the end, he just *knew*. It was like déjà vu, or being reminded of a story you had heard before. It felt right when he heard it.

Perhaps that feeling of rightness was what calmed his anxiety, if only a little, allowing fatigue to take over and the shock of all that had happened to take its toll.

Whatever the case, they were only a few miles down the interstate before Eric had drifted off to sleep.

Raziel gripped the steering wheel tightly as he drove, the tension in his body coiled as he sat next to the boy. The last few years had been a period of gray limbo, filled with meaningless meanderings punctuated by visits from the man he had met outside of Eric's house a lifetime ago. If he had walked through a doorway when he turned away from Eric to pursue that monstrosity in the van, he had locked the door behind him when he had agreed to work for the man who called himself Mr. Teneber. At the time, he had been so full of anger and fear that he had felt it was his only choice. He had kenned the nature of Teneber when he first encountered him, and to his shame, he had been afraid.

So he had agreed to work for the man and that which he served, only gaining a full appreciation for the depth of his mistake in retrospect. He found himself in a paradox of self-loathing now--on the one hand, he hated himself for how short-sighted he had been when aligning himself with an agent of the Darkness. On the other, he truly was beyond redemption now. He now actively worked against the Will of the High, and there was no coming back from that.

Of course, his work was only now beginning in earnest. Over the last few years he had done the occasional task for Teneber, but they were short-lived and fairly innocuous. But this....

Raziel gritted his teeth, focusing on the road as the miles rolled by, trying without success to push away the thoughts that invaded and accused. It was more than betrayal or blasphemy that he was working towards now. The wholesale usurpation and destruction of Creation could be the end result of his fear and defiance. Did he want that stain upon him for eternity? Had he wandered so far from the path of his God that he would participate in such a thing?

Eric stirred slightly in his sleep, shifting against the car door. Raziel looked over at him, his jaw muscle jumping as he regarded the boy. It was *his* fault that any of this had come to pass. Why should he be so special? Why should the High pick this *sack of meat* over one of his most diligent servants? Why didn't the High just stop the Darkness before it began this plan to begin with? But no. Instead, he had set up Raziel to fail and to Fall. All for no reason. All for this *boy*.

He stared back out at a sky that had become faded blue as the day climbed towards noon. He had given his God so much, never questioning. And *this* was his reward. Exile. Damnation.

As much as he feared these things, he feared nothingness more. Even anguish was preferable to the Void. And those were his choices now: damnation or destruction. His only hope in any kind of existence was to align himself with those that would still have him and see that they were victorious. It was a weak and pathetic hope, but it was all that he had.

He glanced back over at Eric, a grim smile ghosting across his lips. Well, he did have one other thing. Revenge.

Chapter Nine

The next three and a half months passed by slowly for Eric, the sharp feelings of fear and anxiety giving away to a kind of dull apathy as he slipped into the routine of his travels. He had attempted to escape several times the first few days, but Raziel never slept, and he would just suddenly *appear* before Eric had gone more than a hundred feet. He still tried sporadically. The last time, they stood at the perimeter of a gas station where they were gassing up, the wind stirring Eric's hair into his eyes as he looked up at Raziel.

Raziel leaned forward, his eyes gleaming with a strange light as he spoke. "I can move quick as a thought, boy. And I can find you wherever you go. You, and your father. I can't harm you--that much is true. But do not think for a moment that curtesy applies to anyone else."

Eric continued to stare up at him, his face hard. "You touch him and I'll kill you."

Raziel laughed. "Sure you will. Just mind me and you won't have to have my murder on your conscience."

That had been three weeks ago in southern Indiana. He still didn't know whether he believed Raziel was what he claimed or not, but either way he felt trapped and unsure of what he should do. For now, he just picked places away from Georgia at random, trying to keep distance from his family while he waited for an opportunity to present itself.

That opportunity came two days later when he pointed down a rural gravel road that led even deeper into the woods of Missouri than they already were. Raziel didn't care where they went, and Eric had seen enough at this point to feel that he probably wouldn't be safe just flagging down a policeman. Whatever Raziel was, he was far too fast and strong to be thwarted easily. It seemed his best bet was to lose himself and hide away from Raziel. If he could get away deep enough into woods, maybe he could work his way out and flag down a ride before Raziel could track him down. Maybe.

Still, it was the best idea he had at the moment. So he pointed down the country road and felt slight relief when Raziel turned onto it without a word. Eric noticed a sign pointing down the direction they were going as they passed, rusty with age nearly to the point of illegibility. He could just make it out before it was gone: Deritus, 5 mi.

The gravel road crunched under the tires as they moved further in the woods. It was only mid-afternoon, but here the day was already losing ground quickly. Trees and bushes pressed in on all sides, darkening the road as it wound and narrowed toward some unknown end.

Then the road widened and the trees thinned, with the crest of the next hill bringing into view a tastefully ornate sign with old-fashioned writing in relief upon the wood. Eric read the sign as they passed by: **Welcome to Deritus, Missouri. Stay Awhile and Watch Us Grow!**

Eric laughed to himself as he read the last, wondering at what point in this town's history did people think it was going to become some sprawling metropolis. As it stood, it seemed to be a small flame of civilization nestled deep in endless miles of dark woods.

Despite this, Eric found himself pleasantly surprised at how picturesque the town was. Street lamps alternated with trees fresh with spring blossoms. Children played in a small park as they drove past, and numerous couples and individuals could be seen going about their business, occasionally stopping to talk with one another.

The town seemed ideal, and it took Eric a moment to place the feeling that was growing in his chest. Dread. A dull and nameless dread that had no apparent source or reason. It was strange, and it seemed all the more peculiar given their surroundings.

He looked over at Raziel, debating whether or not to mention it. Finally he took a deep breath and turned toward his would-be executioner.

"There's something wrong with this place."

Raziel cut his eyes toward him, his lips thinning as he looked back to the road. "Wrong how?"

"I don't know. I just have a bad feeling about this place."

Raziel shrugged. "Could be that's so. There are plenty of bad places in the world, and you'll likely be drawn to them the same as they are to you."

"Drawn to me?"

The man nodded. "Like moths to a giant evil flame."

Eric bristled. "I'm not evil. *You're* the supposed fallen angel."

Raziel snorted but didn't respond. Without another word, he pulled into a parking space on Main Street outside of a restaurant called Just Rite Bites.

"What're you doing? I don't think we should stop here."

"How fortunate that I don't care."

"But..."

Raziel shot him a look, his eyes dark. "Look, it's almost night and we're in the middle of nowhere. Now I don't get tired or need sleep, but I do get bored, and I'm sick of driving. It may be true that this is a bad place, but either way, it doesn't matter much as far as we're concerned. You won't come to harm while I'm with you."

"Until you kill me."

Raziel smiled at him warmly. "Yes, until then. But for tonight we're going to stay right here in beautiful Deritus." He pointed to the restaurant through the windshield. "Now, do you want to eat?"

Eric sighed. "Yeah, I guess so."

Raziel turned off the engine. "Let's go."

The inside of Just Rite Bites was just like the rest of Deritus--beautiful, wholesome and inviting. Every surface was clean and well-maintained, from the steady glow of the neon that was judicially spread throughout to the polished chrome that gilded the counters, barstools, and tables. It reminded Eric of the Fifties-theme diners that he had been in before, but this one seemed the real deal. There were a few people at the booths around the restaurant's perimeter and no one sat at the counter. Without looking back at Raziel, Eric moved to a bar stool and sat down.

As the other man joined him, Eric saw movement from the kitchen. A large paneless window stretched along the wall behind the counter, giving a view into where the food was prepared. He imagined it was the cook he had seen, but then a waitress came out from a swinging door to the left of the window, giving Eric a smile as she approached.

The woman's name tag said "My name is Elia, and I'm here to help!", and she looked to be in her mid-forties, with warm dark eyes that belied her fair complexion. He found himself struck by how attractive she was—her face seemed to glow with an inner radiance, her movements precise in their grace. When she spoke, it was with a rich and melodious voice.

"Hey Hon. What can I get for you two?"

Eric had grown used to Raziel always ordering only a cup of coffee. He waited for him to do so and then ordered a salad. In truth he would have preferred something more substantial, but he didn't entirely trust this place or even this smiling woman. A salad seemed less likely to be subjected to tampering of one sort or another.

You're getting as crazy as he *is.*

Maybe, but he couldn't shake the feeling that they shouldn't be here. He looked around again at the other customers—a table of teenage girls and a pair of old men sat talking amongst themselves. He noticed one of the old men and a couple of the girls casting glances at them and he gave the girls a nodding smile. They looked away quickly and as he turned back around, he found Raziel looking at him.

"You still feel strange about this place?"

"Yeah, I do. Something isn't right here."

Raziel nodded and sighed. "Fine then. We'll leave after we eat."

Eric felt a surge of uncertainty then. His whole reason for picking this route was so he might have a chance to get away from Raziel. It could be that whatever might be wrong with this place could help him get away and cover his tracks. Or it might kill him. If he wasn't just insane.

But he had to work from what he knew, and he knew the man beside him was dangerous and meant to kill him. He had to get away from Raziel, whether he was an angel or a madman.

He shrugged, trying to look nonchalant. "Eh, I'm probably just imagining it. Let's just leave in the morning."

Raziel snorted and drained his coffee. "Fine."

The next few moments passed in silence, with his gaze wandering to the kitchen window and beyond, where Elia was at a cutting board dicing tomatoes at machine gun speed. He watched in amazement as her knife blurred through cucumbers and carrots with an efficiency bordering on the inhuman. That thought took on new meaning as he watched her make her first mistake. She misjudged and the knife fell too close, cutting the tips off of her index and middle fingers.

Eric sucked in a breath as he stared, watching as the waitress calmly retrieved her fingertips and pressed them back to the wounds.

There was no blood. She can't be alive, there was no...

"Here's your salad, Hon." He looked up at her smiling face and swallowed, forcing his gaze back down as he murmured his thanks. As she let go of the plate, he saw her hand. There were red puckered rings on her skin where the knife had cut moments before. Aside from those marks, her hand was whole.

"What's wrong with you?" Raziel was glaring at him.

Eric looked away and began poking at his salad. "Nothing. Just tired."

"Yeah, sitting there like a lump while I drive must be very tiring for you."

Eric grimaced and forced himself to eat a bit of his salad, trying to forget what he had just seen.

When he awoke he felt a surge of panic, thinking that he had slept through the night and missed his chance. Raziel often took walks while he slept, confident in his ability to track Eric down if he tried to leave. He had planned to stay awake and duck into the woods while Raziel was away, and now it was probably too late. They were in a bed and breakfast on the outside of town, and the room had been pitch black when he had apparently drifted off to sleep. Now there was a dim golden light that he first thought must be the approaching morning.

As he mind cleared, however, he looked around and realized he wasn't in his room at all. Instead of a bed, he lay upon a hard wood table, and close walls painted a cheery yellow had been replaced with distant panels of dark wood and row upon row of bookshelves.

A library?

He sat up and saw that he was at the center of a large crowd of people, their faces pallid and sinister in the meager light. He started to ask a question, but it caught in his throat as he saw the waitress from the diner step forward.

"Bet you're kinda wondering what's going on, arentcha, Hon?" She gave him an almost apologetic smile. "Go to bed one place and wake up another."

"The thought had crossed my mind, yeah." As he spoke, he got to his feet, grateful for once that he had nothing but his clothes to sleep in. He was missing his shoes, but otherwise he was dressed. "So what's the deal?"

Elia the waitress giggled behind her hand. "I just love your accent, by the way."

"Thanks, I guess?"

She grew serious again. "But you were asking a serious question, and you'll get a serious answer." Stepping closer to the table, she looked up at him with eyes that glowed softly in the lamplight. "You've seen a little bit of our town, and you can likely see how nice it is. How happy everyone is."

"Yes, it's a very nice town." Raziel was still nowhere to be seen.

She nodded approvingly. "Thank you for saying so. It really is. It's been the same for a long, long time."

"Ya'll are very lucky." There were at least thirty people surrounding him, with at least twelve of those between him and the only visible door.

"We are, we are. But, as with so many things, all of this comes at a price. For us to remain and survive, for our way of life to be protected, we have to have...*help* from those that visit us."

When the punchline came, he found he wasn't all that surprised.

"We need sustenance than only outsiders can provide." She started to lick her lips as she spoke and stopped herself, looking self-conscious.

"You want to eat me?" It was so bizarre that he wanted to laugh--a few years ago he would have. But the eager looks he saw on the faces of those surrounding him killed any humor he saw in the situation.

She looked almost bashful as she ducked her head in a nod. "I'm afraid so. You and your friend when we find him. Even one of us eating will feed all of us, but we do enjoy it so."

She began to climb onto the table, her lips skinning back from her teeth. Others were circling closer as well.

Eric backed up to the center of the table and turned to see a small boy and an old man, perhaps the boy's grandfather, scrabbling onto the table.

The first hand touched him, grasping his ankle. He felt panic flare up in him for a moment, looking into the hungry eyes that swarmed over him. As he kicked away the hand from his leg, he felt a new emotion burn away the panic and fear. Anger. Months of being guarded and threatened by Raziel, and now this. And what had he done to deserve any of it? Nothing, that's what. It was enough. Too much.

Something rose in him then, flooding his senses and filling his chest to bursting. He felt the world stop for a second and then he was in the middle of a silent storm, thick and black.

As quick as it came it was gone, leaving shrieks of fear and a mist of blood in the air. A circle lay around Eric, strewn meat and bone where a dozen people had stood a few seconds before. Femurs lay snapped in two, skulls nestled in mounts of wet flesh like shattered bird eggs. Some of the gore lay upon the table itself, its wood unblemished by any mark.

The remaining people were terrified, their eyes rolling like frightened cows as they put distance between themselves and where he stood. He was about to try and make a break for it, but just then the doors crashed open. Raziel came charging in, three men hanging from him as he moved. He was bloody in spots, the men striking at his flesh with their mouths as he continued forward.

Eric saw that Raziel's flesh healed back completely within moments of each wound, leaving only time for the barest streams of blood to trickle down. The angel threw off two of the men, but five more surged atop Raziel almost immediately. He bore their weight as he continued to fight, but they stopped his advance for the moment.

Dozens more people had poured into the library from behind Raziel, and now they were all attacking him savagely even as he tossed away their brethren. Within seconds, Eric could only glimpse the angel under the swarming mass of people.

Watching all of this, Eric made his choice quickly. He raised his voice, hoping he sounded confident. Flinging out his hand, he pointed to Raziel as he spoke.

"You see what you have there? A neverending buffet. Keep him as my gift to you." He paused to let this sink in before continuing. He had the attention of all those not currently fighting Raziel. "As for me, I'm leaving now. I hope ya'll know what a deal this is and don't decide to get greedy. Because you've seen what I did to these others, and I have no problem with turning every fucking one of you into paste."

He jumped off the table without waiting for a response, feeling relief wash over him as they stepped back, parting the way. Anger still surged through him, but it was now warring with fear and confusion. He believed he had somehow been responsible for the black mass that had swirled around him, but he knew he had no control over it. Even if he could call it forth again, he wouldn't. It had to have sprung from the thing Raziel called the Darkness. For all he knew, another episode like the one a second ago could bring the Darkness into the world, and he was far more afraid of that than these monsters.

He started walking, fighting the weakness in his legs as he moved into the parted crowd. To his left he saw Raziel struggling under a mass of bodies. As he got even with him, the angel flung off several people and bellowed out to him.

"You leave me and I'll find you. You *and* yours. You know I will."

Eric kept walking, calling out over his shoulder as he walked out. "Maybe that's so. If you do, maybe you'll wish you hadn't."

He slammed the door behind him and leaned against it, puffing out a breath. He saw there were a few people standing outside the library as well, but they somehow seemed to know what had transpired within. They gave him a wide berth, making it easier to make his way back to the street.

In ten minutes he was back at their room. After vomiting in the bathroom at the end of the hall, he washed his face and looked through their room, finding the car keys in the angel's cast-off coat. Raziel's arrogance to the rescue again.

By the time the sun began to rise he was back out on the highway, and by nine he was heading into Kansas.

Lawrence wheeled himself into the spacious bedroom, steam following him like a cloud as he left the bathroom. It had required a great deal of modification to the house and some training on his own part, but he had become quite skilled at caring for himself, including his personal hygiene. Baths were still among the most difficult tasks, if only because of his fastidious attention to detail. On days like today, of course, it transcended precision to become a glorious ritual.

He moved to his bed and took up the additional towel that was folded neatly there, drying himself again before sliding onto the bed. He dressed himself quickly, slipping on underwear and a crisp new dress shirt, the sleeves rolled up to the elbows. They always had to be burned afterward, but he did like to look his best for his guests.

Next came the pants, well-tailored but loose-fitting so as to accommodate the contortions that were about to come. He could feel nothing below his waist, but he didn't want the slightest risk that his movement might be hindered. Then came the sling—made of pliant black leather, it was essentially a large bag which he slid over his lower half. His legs were folded up neatly and tucked away inside the bag while straps at the bag's top ran across his shoulders and back to ensure the apparatus didn't slip or come free.

When he had checked every aspect of his attire, he slid to the head of the bed, easily carried on his arms. He was nearly fifty-eight, but he was stronger now than he had ever been in his life. While his legs had grown atrophied and desiccated over the years, his arms and torso had thickened with cords of hard muscle. Looking at his large hands, it might appear that they were incapable of dexterity or speed, but that was far from the case. With one swift movement he plucked his dentures out and dropped them in the glass of water set aside for that very purpose. He ran his tongue over the metal hidden underneath his false teeth. The wide strips of metal ran along the outer surface of his gums, surgically fused with the bone fourteen years before. As his tongue traveled along the hard, cool surface, he could feel each hole that had been precisely placed in that metal. The dental surgeon had done an excellent job after all--the man's final work had been his best, which was how it should be.

He turned to look lovingly at the rectangular case which sat upon the table beside his bed, running his thumbs over the black polished wood as his heart began to quicken.

A flip of the latch and the box opened slowly, revealing an interior plush with red silk and filled with eighteen molded indentions. Within each indention lay a small piece of black metal. His true teeth.

Each tooth was a work of art—handcrafted according to his specifications and precise in every detail. The form of the metal itself was identical in all eighteen, with each being a cone of sharply-tipped metal just larger than an average human tooth and the base of the cone ending in a downward-thrusting screw. Every tooth was made of a single piece of metal and was extraordinarily strong. There was not an aspect of the teeth that was not beautiful to him.

Of course, their most magnificent feature were the carvings that wrapped around each tooth, traced in silver against the black and written in a language he could not read but which was written upon his heart and soul. The language of his god.

He picked up the first tooth gingerly, enjoying its weight and strength. Careful not to cut himself on its razor point, he slipped his hand into his mouth, lining the tooth up with its hole in the metal of his mouth and screwing it in snuggly. He did the same with each tooth in turn, every movement marked by the grace of practice and the slowness of holy ritual.

When he was finished, he touched his teeth lightly with his tongue and closed his mouth, the tiny metal knives sliding together perfectly to form a black and silver nightmare. His head swam in with excitement as he slid back to the foot of his bed and maneuvered into the chair.

He slipped on black leather gloves from his chair's side pocket and moved to the doorway. He couldn't keep his guest waiting any longer.

Amber regretted coming here. She had doubted the wisdom of taking this 'job' from the very beginning, but she needed the money desperately. She paced around the room for what seemed like the hundredth time, wondering again if she could just ask to go back home. Probably, but what about the money?

She had circled around to the room's full-length mirror again and stopped to study herself. At thirty-three, she was still very attractive. Auburn hair spilled to her tan shoulders, glowing softly in the room's light and framing a heart-shaped face that was very pretty if not beautiful. She had been a low-tier model once, doing a few catalogs and local fashion shows. But if she was honest, she had never really been successful, and the meager living she had made at her dream had dried up over two years ago. She had gotten by since then, working a few odd jobs and relying on the men she dated. But this—what was this she was doing, exactly?

They called it being an 'event escort', describing it as simply being an accessory to a wealthy man who needed a date for a museum gala. That sounded all very nice, and it certainly had appeared to be legitimate so far. A limo had come by for her early this afternoon, and she had gasped when she saw the house they were approaching. It was enormous, easily overshadowing any house she had ever seen, even those on television. Deep in the midst of a massive wooded estate, she felt for a moment as if she had stumbled into a fairy tale. Then her doubts had assailed her again, making her question what would really be expected of her.

She smoothed the front of the evening gown she had been given, marveling again at the delicacy of the deep blue fabric. Her eyes moved up to the sapphire necklace that rested in the hollow of her throat. It had to be real, didn't it? All of this was real. And why go to all this trouble if all they wanted was....

A whore. If all they wanted was a whore.

That was her fear. That regardless of the nice house and dress, regardless of the party that may or may not exist, regardless of all she had seen, that it was all pretense to dress up a rich man's whoring. The only thing that frightened her more was that she might not say no if she were offered enough.

She began to cry softly and turned away from the mirror in a panic. She mustn't ruin her make up, or it...

The lights went out. The curtains had been drawn tightly since she had been told to wait in the room, but it had passed from dusk into nightfall in the interim, and there was no light left to peek from around the edges of the windows. She was in total darkness.

Her heart hammering in her chest, she began to move slowly along the wall in the direction she remembered the door being. She stubbed her toe once in the process and nearly knocked over a heavy vase as she went, but she finally reached the door. It was locked.

She cursed under her breath as her fear continued to build, and she gave out a small yelp as she heard another door open and then quickly shut somewhere in the room. The thought flashed through her mind that she didn't remember seeing another door in the room, but then she heard the dragging sound and the idea fled her mind.

The sound was soft and rhythmic--*shush....shush....shush...shush...*--she found it hard to pinpoint its source in the dark. Moving toward the center of the room, she winced at the sound of her own footfalls. Then she was on the large rug that covered much of the room and was able to move silently. Her plan was to move toward where she had heard the second door open, her hope being that once she had located it she would find it unlocked. She had no thought of crying out for help; the small part of her brain that was guarding her survival knew this had all been arranged and that silence was her best friend.

Then she realized she no longer heard the sound of movement in the room. Either whatever it was had stopped...or it was on the rug as well. Which meant it could be anywhere.

Strong hands gripped both of her ankles simultaneously, yanking Ashley swiftly to the ground. She attempted to get up right away, but she was borne down by the weight of someone crawling up her length. As panic threatened to block out all thought, she rolled onto her back in a desperate attempt to dislodge her attacker. But she felt the person moving with her roll, ending up on top of her chest when she landed on her back.

She heard a deep and strange voice yell, "Lights!" and the next moment the lights were on again and she was looking into the face of the Devil. Eyes of electric blue blazed in a twisted mask of hate hard with age and malice. Then her eyes found its mouth—black and sharp, the thing clicked its teeth at her before barking out a laugh. She had time to think the teeth must be metal before they sank into her cheek.

Lindsay grimaced at the heat of the plates as she took them quickly to table four, her hands aching as she gave the couple at the table a quick smile before heading back to the kitchen. This was the busiest time at the diner, the time when she always felt as though she was running behind. She knew she could carry more and get burned less if she used trays like the other girls, but she honestly lacked the balance to do it without pitching half her cargo on a customer or the floor.

She had taken the job five weeks before out of desperation, having arrived a few days earlier in Kansas City without any real reason to be there. She had left Georgia six months ago with the idea of going somewhere new and exciting. Her feeling of dissatisfaction with herself and her life had gradually grown since she was attacked over three and a half years ago, culminating in her exodus from Georgia and her new determination to find whatever it was she seemed to be missing.

But with time, she realized that she had no inkling what the source of her unhappiness was, and the thrill of travel had waned after countless bus rides and uncomfortable nights. She still would have been happy pursuing her goal despite all of this if she had not realized the truth. She had no idea what she wanted or who she wanted to be. She only knew that she didn't like herself or her life as they were.

It seemed to Lindsay that everything had slowed and faded since then, her weak hopes of finding something more or better guttering as she left the Southeast and eventually stopped in Missouri. Broke and hopeless, she had taken the first job she had seen.

So here I am, the wonderfully inept waitress.

Still, she was lucky to have the job and she knew it. The pay was terrible, but far from the worst she had seen. And if Patrick was a little grabby with his hands from time to time, he was still fairly laidback and amiable. All in all, things could be much worse.

She snorted softly, thinking that it was the sign of a desperate life when every moment needed to be compared to a worse case scenario to have any merit. Refilling several coffee cups, she glanced at the clock that buzzed softly from its place high on the wall above the booths. Twelve-forty. Another two hours or so to go.

Lindsay was in good enough shape and the diner was small enough that most days didn't exhaust her, but busy or slow, the work was so *dull*. Sure, she got to meet people, but after a few days she realized that most of the people that came to the diner were regulars. Regulars often meant bigger tips, but they also meant more talking. An assumed familiarity that wasn't there. More effort than she really wanted to give anyone, including herself.

She heard her name called and groaned inwardly, knowing that one of the regulars must be low on coffee or want to tell her another story. One she had no doubt heard before.

When she turned, she nearly dropped the coffee pot, only saving it by slamming it to the counter as she took three steps towards the booth where a large man sat. The man was young, but it was hard to tell his exact age due to his appearance. He was possibly the sickest looking person she had ever seen. His coat drawn up as he shivered, he looked out at her with hazy eyes from underneath a sweat-sheened brow.

"Lindsay? Is that you?" He looked as if he was trying to rise, but it was clear he was too weak to do so.

Her mind raced as she tried to make sense of it all, fumbling for any less extraordinary answer for this man being here. Ultimately she could think of no logical reason for the coincidence and accepted it as it was.

"You're....you're the guy that saved my life."

He nodded halfheartedly, his eyes lowered. His head bobbed and swayed with the effort and he blinked as if trying to stay awake. "Linds...Lindsay...I'm sick...I can't die...Don't let..." Eric trailed off as he tumbled out of the booth and onto the floor, whispering her name one more time before spasming and growing still.

Part II: Pattern

Chapter Ten

The world swam into focus like a mermaid's dream--full of deep, shimmering blues and cool promises of light. Eric dove up and out, out of the black and into a familiar field he had never seen before. The grass was long and flowing, rolling like waves around the lone tree which stood a few yards away. It took only a glimpse for him to recognize his mother sitting under that tree. He moved to her, his confusion stopping him short.

"Mama? You're dead, aren't you?"

She nodded and grinned. "Always were a bright boy." She laughed and nodded again. "I surely am. And you're not far behind if something doesn't change soon."

He winced as a pain shot through his head, causing him to cry out. When he looked up, his mother looked concerned, all but the smallest glimmer of laughter gone from her eyes. "What do you mean?"

"Don't you remember?"

He sat down in the grass a few feet from her, still rubbing his temples. "I remember....Well, I remember crossing over into Kansas. I was already feeling bad then, and in a bit I was feeling a lot worse. Real sick. Then I felt a strong urge to go back...not to that damned town, but just back the other way. I didn't know where I was going. Just following the roads and turning when it felt right. Before I knew it I was near Kansas City. I don't remember much after that."

The woman sighed and leaned back on her hands, looking up at the sky while she spoke. "You're dying, Eric. Being killed by the thing inside you, the thing you used to kill those horrible creatures that were trying to get you in Deritus."

He leaned forward, his fists clenched. "I can't die! If I die, Raziel says it'll come across...it'll kill everything. I...how can I stop it?"

She turned away from the sky to look at him. "You're not meant to die. You're only dying because you're resisting the thing that rose in you before. That kind of power...it's going to take a toll on you regardless. A human person isn't meant for that kind of thing. But it's you fighting it that's making things worse."

Eric's eyes narrowed. "Who are you? You're not my mother."

"I never said I was, did I? Do you think any of this is real?"

"*Who are you?*"

"When you say it all stern like that I just want to tell you all the secrets of the universe, Eric."

He leapt to his feet, determined to put as much distance between himself and this impostor as he could. But before he could turn she spoke again.

"I'm not lying to you, Eric. Deep down you know I'm not."

He gritted his teeth and turned away, his head down as he walked toward the edge of the field where a stone fence ran off into the distance in both directions. "So I'm supposed to just buy what you're saying and give into the Darkness?"

"Boy, if the Darkness wanted you dead, why would it save you in Deritus?"

Eric stopped and listened.

"If you're going to die for its cause, apparently it wants it to be a bit down the line. Either way, it's what saved you before, and your fighting it is what's killing you now."

"So what if I stop fighting it? It'll just take me over?"

"Doesn't work like that. It'll be the same as before. You might even gain some control over when you use it. With time, that is."

He spun around, glaring at the woman. "I don't ever want to use it again. *Ever.*"

She shrugged. "What we want and what will be are very different things most times. There are going to be many obstacles in your path. You're going to have to call on that power again sooner or later." She stood up slowly, stretching her back. "But that's for later. For now, you best go back to sleep with your head on straight. Do that and you might just pull through. Nighty-night, Eric."

"Eric!"

He was remotely aware of opening one eye and the world exploding into painful light. Squinting his eyes closed, he realized that he was being shaken by a hand on his shoulder. His body was leaden, so it took time for him to stir his lips enough to mumble, "What is it?"

"You were having a nightmare I guess. Thrashing around. I was afraid you were going to have another seizure." The voice was young and feminine. He heard her concern clearly, and it caused his head to swim with different emotions as he struggled to open his eyes again. He saw an unfamiliar room—someone's bedroom. Then he saw her and remembered. Lindsay.

"Where are we?" He raised his head and looked at her more properly, his heart thudding as she looked down on him, her face filled with relief and smiling now.

"My house. I took you to my house. You woke up after you collapsed at the diner, just for a few seconds. You told me no hospital. They gave me a fit, but I convinced my boss that you were my brother and that you had seizures a lot. Convinced him a little at least."

His throat felt dry and constricted as he spoke, his tongue a lump of unwieldy meat. "Thank you. Thank you....for helping me."

"Hey, it's not everyday you get to help the man who saved your life from a whacked-out serial killer."

"I didn't really..."

She patted his arm. "You can impress me with your modesty later. Go back to sleep for now. We'll talk when you wake up. Unless you need something now?"

Eric was already asleep.

Chapter Eleven

He wolfed down the food before him, Lindsay refilling his plate with more eggs and toast twice before he finally began to slow down. As he ate he would occasionally remember that she was watching him as she picked at her own food, and he would look up to give her a brief, sheepish smile before diving back in. Finally he leaned back in his chair, taking a deep breath as he wiped his mouth on a paper towel.

"Man. Thanks so much for that. I guess I was really hungry."

She laughed, an easy laugh that made him smile for no real reason, and pointed a thumb at the tiny kitchen a few feet away. "You sure you don't want any more? I think I'm out of eggs, but I can probably spit a pig for you or something."

He shook his head. "No, if I ate anymore I'd probably pass out again." He paused at this and looked away before continuing. "Thank you again for helping me. I'm sorry for bothering you like this."

"Bother? Are you kidding? It's not your fault you got sick and it's sure no bother. You *saved my life*, remember? I'm just amazed that we ran into each other all the way out here. Talk about fate, huh?"

Eric felt his stomach squirm at the mention of fate and stood to take his plate to the sink. Since waking an hour before, he had felt perfectly fine, with all signs of his prior sickness having vanished. While that was good news, it was far from all he had to worry about.

"Don't worry about that, I'll get it."

He shook his head. "My mama raised me better than that. I'll do the dishes. It's the least I can do."

She started to stand up. "Seriously, you're just getting better and..."

"No, I've got it. I'm fine now." She sat down again. He wondered if he had sounded too harsh. He was a total stranger after all, and he didn't want to frighten her. Despite what she said, she didn't really owe him anything.

He scrubbed at the dishes, unable to push away his fears, especially the thoughts of Raziel popping up at any moment to take him away and possibly hurt Lindsay in the process. The one good thing he had ever done was helping her, and he was about to ruin it by putting her in danger.

Drying the dishes she had brought over while he washed, Eric turned toward her. He realized that she had just sat quietly while he was at the sink, as if she sensed that he had needed the time to think and sort something out. Now he knew what he needed to do.

"Lindsay...You've been great, and I can't ever repay you for your kindness and um, your hospitality. But I've got to go today. Right now in fact." He expected an immediate response--perhaps a semi-sincere "No, you should stay a bit longer" and then quick acceptance. Instead, the girl just sat calmly sipping her juice, her eyes distant as if she were the one in deep thought now. He dried his hands quietly and waited, looking at her.

He was struck again by how pretty she was. Or perhaps attractive was a better word. Because while she was certainly beautiful with her dark eyes and fair skin, he was drawn to her as much or more because of her presence. She was clearly intelligent and had a strong personality--he could tell this from only a hour's conversation. And this was a large part of what made her stand out so. But at the same time it was something more indefinable as well. She just seemed more *real* than most people. More there. When she was nearby in perception or thought, everything else seemed to pale slightly, receding into the background.

Weirdo. You really are going to wind up being a whack job before this is all over. And then, *It won't be over until I'm dead.*

Maybe so. And all the more reason to leave now rather than endanger Lindsay any further. He was about to speak up when she beat him to it.

"Who's Raziel?" The girl paused and let the question hang for a moment before continuing. "You talked a lot the last few hours you were asleep. Who or what is Raziel? It is a who, isn't it?" She still held her glass of juice in her hand, her eyes still distant as she listened for his answer.

He put the towel down and started towards the table. "Look, Lindsay, it'll be better if I just..."

She turned toward him, her gaze pinning him to the spot. "Answer the question, Eric. If you want to thank me, then be honest with me."

He eased forward and sank back into his chair at the table. "Look, what difference does it make? I have to leave. I'm putting you in danger staying here."

Her gaze was unwavering as she sat her glass down and leaned forward. "Just tell me, okay? Payment for my kindness."

Eric sighed and nodded, dropping his eyes. "Okay, okay. He's a guy, yes. A very bad guy who's after me. He had me before. Kidnapped me a few months ago. He's obsessed with me I guess you could say." He picked up the paper towel he had left at the table and began to twist it. "He's crazy. Crazy and dangerous."

She didn't react as he thought she would. He could see her taking it all in out of the corner of his eye and then she asked another question. Not "have you called the police" or "why is he after you", but "Well, do you think he'll find you again?"

He shrugged, forcing himself to meet her eyes again. "I don't know. I honestly don't know. Probably. He's very good at finding me. I wouldn't have gotten away this time, but he had gotten jumped by a group of guys and was distracted."

She nodded. "Well, maybe they took care of him. Put him in the hospital or killed him." She didn't sound as if she had any problem with either scenario.

He shook his head, dropping the gnarled paper towel as he turned to look out a nearby window. "No, he won't get beat. Not by them. They may slow him down, or even trap him for awhile, but he'll be too much for them in the end. Then he'll get out and he'll come for me."

"What aren't you telling me about all of this?"

He laughed bitterly, feeling a flare of anger toward this girl. What right did she have to pry into any of this? It wasn't her business, and she thought she wanted to know but she had no clue. She'd think he was crazy if he told her everything. She was just stubborn and willful and...

She reached out and gave his hand a squeeze, her eyes sad as she smiled at him. "I'm not trying to be pushy. But I owe you my life, and besides that, I really like you. You're a really nice guy. I can see that. But you're in trouble. Bad trouble. I can see that too. Please let me help."

He felt something tug in his chest and he fought it down. *No. I'm not going to be selfish and give in to her sympathy. Get her killed. Haven't I caused enough pain for people?* He clenched his jaw and stood. "Look, I've got to go."

"I've got terminal cancer."

He felt his head go light and he sat down again, his strings cut. He looked at her and tried to find a way to respond that didn't sound stupid and insensitive. He felt a new burst of anger, this time at himself. Why hadn't he had a flash, any sense at all, of her condition? His supposed 'power' was worthless, incapable of actually helping people. He supposed he couldn't expect more from something born of evil, but he still felt guilt and disappointment weighing him down as he asked his stupid question.

"You do?"

She nodded. "I found out three months ago. It's metastasized, and the doctor said I have about six to nine months left to live." She paused and frowned. "Um, well, I guess it's three to six now."

His face fell as he felt his eyes growing watery. "God. I'm...I'm so sorry. I don't know what to say. How are you doing?"

She smiled. "No ill effects so far. Apparently it won't affect me much until the last few weeks. I've still got some good time in me. Time to live my life."

He wiped at his eyes and nodded. "What can I do for you? How can I help you?"

She looked at him for a moment, her own eyes misting for a second before she blinked and looked away, shaking her head. "My God, you really are just *good*, aren't you?"

He frowned and shook his head. "No I'm not. I...No, this isn't about me. How can I help you?"

She looked at him and swallowed, her eyes clear. "Stay with me. Just for awhile."

"Lindsay, I can't. It's too dang—"

"Look, what do I care if this nutjob comes or not? If he does we'll call the police, and even if he killed me in my sleep, I'm not exactly going to be worse off than suffering a lingering death in a few months, am I?"

"But you don't..."

"I don't understand? I know I don't know all of what's going on. You've got more that you don't want to tell me, at least not yet, and I'm okay with that. But what I do know is that we both need help, and I think we can help each other. For a little while at least."

He started to shake his head again but she stopped him.

"Don't shake your head at me. I don't have anything to lose, and I want you here, okay?"

"But why? You don't even know me. And you don't know what Raziel is capable of. I don't either, really, but I don't want to risk you getting hurt."

"It's my choice and my risk. And I may not know you yet, but I want to."

"I..." He didn't know what to do. Listening to her arguments, he felt himself slowly giving in and trying to believe everything she was saying. She was so earnest and passionate when she spoke, her eyes fiery and her voice strong but not unkind. And to be wanted...to be cared for...it had been so long since he had felt worth the trouble. It felt wonderful.

But for all of that, it was a lie. A pretty lie that he would be telling himself if he bought into all of this. It would be selfish of him to put her in jeopardy, despite all she had said. She was a stranger who had no idea what she was getting involved in. He couldn't risk it.

She reached out and touched his arm. "Please stay for a little while. Take it a day at a time." Her eyes searched his own and he felt everything fading into the background.

He swallowed and nodded. "Okay. A day at a time."

Bastard. Selfish fucking bastard.

Chapter Twelve

A day became two, which became one week and then another. Eric had enough money to help pay for things for a little while, but it wasn't long before he knew he would have to get a job of some sort if he was going to keep contributing. Of course, that was never what he told himself. Every day he told himself that tomorrow was his last day with Lindsay, that he would tell her that night or perhaps just leave while she was gone during the day. When the money ran low, he told himself that he took a job at the diner washing dishes to build back up his traveling money so he could leave in a day or two. When he spent the money helping Lindsay pay for groceries, he told himself that he would get paid again in a few days and then he could just go. That this time he *would* go.

During all of this he spent his lunches and all his breaks with the girl who had taken him in so freely. He went home with her at night and the hours seemed to fly by, watching movies and talking. On the weekends she would take him around the city, almost as much of a tourist as he was. The entire time he was completely comfortable with her, and she seemed to feel the same.

As the days passed, he felt himself having to fight harder and harder to not touch her or try to kiss her. She had never tried anything herself, or given any indication one way or the other of how she looked at him. But he knew that none of it mattered. He couldn't stay forever, and she would be gone before much longer. It would be pointless and unnecessarily painful for both of them to start something romantic.

As he sat with her at lunch nearly a month after he had collapsed in the diner, he watched her laughing at his lame jokes and realized for the hundredth time how stupid he had been.

"What do you want to do tonight?" She gave him her quirked smile and tilted her head, making him flush slightly as he took off his apron and shrugged.

"Whatever you want. You sure you're not sick of me hanging around yet?"

She shook her head and held open the kitchen's swinging door, making an ushering motion while she bowed dramatically. "Not at all, good sir. Not at all."

He walked out and laughed. "You're really odd, you know it?"

She grinned at him and nodded. "Yep. It's part of my charm, you know?"

"You think?"

She smiled at him again, her eyes twinkling. "Don't you?"

He swallowed and headed outside without answering, looking around as he waited for her to lock up. However foolish he may have become, he still knew that a threat was out there. His eyes adjusted to the shadows and he couldn't see anything in them, but he knew that meant little. He felt the constant thread of guilt that had run through his days with Lindsay thicken and twine around his heart as it had so many times before, but then he felt her hands on his shoulders, shaking him gently, and he turned to see her smiling up at him.

"Wake up. Why don't you take me out to dinner?"

He laughed. "Where at? It's one in the morning. The only places open are places like this."

She shook her head. "Wrong wrong. All-night Chinese downtown."

"You want to go all the way downtown now?"

"You got a better offer?"

He laughed again. "Come on."

"The key is noodles. If you trace any Chinese dish back to its basic components, you'll find noodles."

Eric raised an eyebrow. "Um, that makes no sense whatsoever."

"No, seriously. I defy you to name a Chinese food that does not contain noodles to some degree."

"Fried dumplings."

Lindsay waved her hand dismissively. "Dumplings are just big noodles. They take the big noodles, wrap them up pretty, and fry 'em. That's all."

"Yeah, I really don't think so."

"It's true. Give me another."

He grinned at her. "Pork-fried rice."

"Rice is where noodles come from. They're like baby noodles."

"Noodles are like eggs and flour or something. Not rice."

"No, I'm afraid it's rice. I've read a study on it." She lifted her head dismissively and took a sip from her drink.

"Uh, yeah." He smiled to the waitress as she brought out their order. The restaurant was easily one of the strangest he had ever been in. It looked to have once been a fast-food restaurant, but it had now been turned into one of the most dubious looking late-night eateries he had ever seen. But Lindsay had sworn by it, having tried it a few weeks earlier, and when he dug in, he was surprised to find that the food was actually quite good.

They ate for a few minutes in comfortable silence, and then she put down her fork. "Why is that guy after you?"

He swallowed his current bite of food, his stomach plummeting. Tomorrow marked the end of the fourth week since he had come to stay with Lindsay, and in all that time, she had never brought up Raziel or anything related to him in all. Eric had been grateful for that. He knew he couldn't expect her to believe him if he told her the truth, despite how close it seemed they had grown in the last month. It sounded too crazy. It *was* too crazy.

"It's complex."

She pushed her plate back and looked at him seriously, lacing her fingers before her as she took a deep breath and appeared to make the decision to push on.

"That's okay. I can handle complex."

"Look, I just don't think..."

"No, *you* look. You've got some kook who's stalking you, who's...casting a shadow over every day of your life. And I haven't asked anything about it because I felt it wasn't any of my business. But now I'm starting to think that maybe it *is* some of my business, and I'd like to know if you'll tell me."

He frowned. "'Casting a shadow'?...Look I don't know what you're talking about. I just had some trouble with a guy, and he might still be out there. But I'm not worried about it."

"That's bullshit. Don't you think I see how you look over your shoulder all the time? How you always tense when we're outside? That's no way to live." She licked her lips and continued on before he could respond. "Before I was born, my dad had an accident. It cost the family a lot, and he was never the same after it. Growing up, he always worried me. He drank a lot by the time I got in school, and he would look at me funny sometimes."

She paused and then blurted out in a whisper. "He never touched me or anything. I didn't even really know about that stuff back then. But I guess I knew enough to worry. I wouldn't let myself be alone with him if I could help it, and I always felt a weight on my back when I thought about him. A gloom that followed me around all the time."

Lindsay wiped at her eyes and let out a short, bitter laugh. "It was kind of a relief when he died, you know? I cried for like two weeks straight, but part of me was glad. Because I didn't have to worry anymore."

He started to reach out and stopped himself, letting his hand fall to the table. "When did he die?"

She shrugged, wiping her nose with a paper napkin. "I was still a child. He had been working as a bank security guard at the time, and there was a robbery. He got shot trying to stop the robbers."

Eric felt his gorge rising as he gripped the edge of the table, trying to look calm as the color faded from everything in the room. "The robbers...they got away?"

"Well, one did, though he got caught a few minutes later. The other two got killed at the bank. My dad had gotten one of them, and the other got accidentally shot by his partner or something. Apparently there was a big newspaper article about it at the time. Because it was so weird. I didn't find out the details until I was in high school. I looked up the old newspapers in the library...what's wrong?"

"Lindsay...I've got to leave. Tomorrow. I can't put you in any more danger."

Her eyes went wide. "Danger? What're you talking about? It's been a month and there's been no sign of this guy. If you're worried, let's go to the police."

Eric was already shaking his head. "No, it's not that. Well, it is that, but it's other stuff too. More stuff than I can explain. I just need you to trust me that I have to go."

He almost jerked back in surprise when she gently grabbed his chin, looking into his eyes with a slight smile. "I do trust you. I have from the start. But you're not leaving me. If you go, I'm going with you."

Now he did jerk back. "Lindsay, no. I'm not joking here. I wish things were different. God, I do. Meeting you has been more than...well, things aren't different. None of it matters, okay? I have to go in the morning. I'm not going to have your death on my hands."

Lindsay's face darkened as he spoke. He had barely finished his last word before she started in again. "'My death on your hands'? It's not your choice to make, is it? I'm going to die soon anyway, or don't you remember? And last time I checked, I wasn't a child to be patted on the head and sent on her little way. You're in trouble. I get that. And I want to help you if I can. And if I can't, I still want to be with you. Can you tell me you don't want to be with me?"

She wasn't going to let this go. She would keep on and on until he caved. It wouldn't be hard when he wanted to stay so much. Unless he ended it now.

He made his voice hard and hoped his face didn't betray the lie. "What are we even doing here? You want to be with me? What the fuck are you talking about? Do you think we've got a romance going here? You're *dying*. I may not want a long-term relationship, but come on, I don't want a corpse either. Let's just cut our losses, okay? I'll leave tonight."

Fresh tears sprang into her eyes, his chest feeling as if it might cave in at any second as he forced himself to keep looking at her. "Fuck you, Eric. *Fuck you.* Do you think I'm stupid or something? Do you think you can pull the 'you're a bad dog, Lassie' bit on me? I know you. *I know you already.* And you're full of shit."

"I'm being serious."

"So am I, big boy. Answer my question. Do you want to leave without me? Tell me."

He gritted his teeth as he slowly shook his head from side to side. "You're not being fair."

"Never claimed to be fair. Tell me."

He shot her a dark look. "No, okay? No, I don't want to be without you. Are you happy?"

"Not yet. Will you stay or let me go with you? Whatever you think is best. Safest."

"Damn it. Fine. I'll stay. For a bit longer, at least."

She smiled, paying no mind to the orphan tear that trickled down her cheek. "Then I'm happy. For a bit longer, at least."

Laying in the dark on the living room sofa, hours after Lindsay had gone to bed, he stared up into the moonlight and breathed in the salty taste of his tears. He had been silently crying for awhile now, his mind a tilting storm of thought and emotion. It had all gone too far now. Before he realized it, it was all too late.

He wasn't going to leave her. He would stay until the end, taking care of her when the cancer got bad. Making her as happy as he could. Ignoring the monstrosity that lay coiled in the shadow of his soul, waiting to overtake him. Trying to forget the fallen angel that wanted to kill him so. And resigning himself to doing whatever he had to in order to protect Lindsay.

If Raziel came near her, he would rip him apart.

Chapter Thirteen

The park was slightly more crowded than Lindsay would have liked, but she couldn't blame other people for taking advantage of what had been a beautiful day so far. After spending the morning walking around shops at the Plaza, she had taken Eric over to the park for lunch. Now he was over buying them some candy at a store across the street, and she had every idea that he was watching out the window the entire time.

The Chinese restaurant had been three days ago, and she was still uncertain if it had solved anything. For the short-term, maybe. But eventually...

She sighed and looked out at the duck pond that was nearby. Usually the happy quacking noises would make her smile, but she was finding it hard to stay cheerful. She hadn't had any choice. She had believed it at the time, and she still believed it now. It had felt right. She hoped she hadn't made a mistake.

When she had seen Eric the day he had passed out, she had spent some time questioning the odds of running into him like that. After he had awoken, after only a few words, she had known she wanted to get to know him better. When he started talking about leaving, she had been filled with an instant and unreasoning fear that she couldn't explain or understand.

She thought she understood it now. Eric was the best person she had ever met. He had a calm and gentle way about him that soothed her, and he never missed anything it seemed. He was always listening and thinking, sometimes nodding to himself as if remembering things long forgotten. She doubted he even realized he did it.

He would tell jokes and laugh at hers, but never his own. And he always listened to her like it was the only thing he could ever think of doing. He was kind without trying. He...he was afraid.

She hadn't lied when she said she already knew him. She didn't know him entirely, but she knew a lot. She knew he was no coward. Far from it. And he was terrified of whatever lay behind him and what might lie ahead. It worried and frightened her, but she didn't know what to do other than wait and try to help when the time came.

But for all her hopes and plans, she still worried the most about what she *knew* would come eventually. She didn't want to lose him.

"Ma'am, I believe you ordered the peanut variety?"

She smiled up at him, her heart quickening. "I did, good sir. Now come enjoy the beautiful view with me."

Eric sat down, his eyes warm as he grinned at her. "This was a really good idea. I'm having a great time."

Then he was gripping his head, his candy dropped and scattered across the grass. He winced, palms pressed against his temples even as she reached out in concern.

"Eric, what is it? What's the matter?"

He looked up at her, his pupils huge and black as he gasped, "He's coming. He's coming."

She looked around, panic shooting through her like a shock. "Who, the guy? Raziel? Where?"

He shook his head, still breathing heavy. "No...Not him. The other."

Eric tried to get to his feet, but it was too much. He was awash in sensation, a jumble of images and feelings that made no sense to him making his head fill like a bag of broken glass. He didn't know what the words he had spoken meant, but he knew they were true. Then a deep, masculine voice called out from very nearby and he looked up, his confusion and dread mounting.

"Ah, here you both are. How nice. It really is a beautiful day, isn't it?"

Lindsay turned to look as well, irritation on her face. Then she saw the man before them and her face fell slightly, as if she knew. Perhaps she did.

It wasn't anything in his appearance. He was a rather small man and far from imposing in his crisply pressed white suit and dapper matching hat. Eric had the random thought that they were called fedoras, but he couldn't have said for certain. The man certainly looked out of place, anachronistic enough to be just a step on this side of surreal. But for all that, he looked harmless enough.

But he was far from it. Eric could feel menace baking off this man, this *thing*, like a deep and sullen heat. It was like watching a snake in a baby's crib. It was only a matter of time.

And yet.

And yet he didn't feel wholly surprised by the man. Nor was he truly afraid of him, though he knew his arrival would only bring something bad. In fact, this man with his quick, unpleasant eyes and too-smooth face seemed somewhat familiar to Eric, and that *did* frighten him.

All of these thoughts tumbled through Eric's head in a lightning torrent, the small man staring down at him with a smile that concealed a great deal of irony and arrogance beneath a thin layer of artificial warmth. In that moment he realized that he truly disliked this man, whatever would come from their meeting and whoever or whatever he may be.

"Who are you?" Eric's words came out in a whisper, strong but low as he focused his eyes on the stranger's.

"I am called Mr. Teneber. I am an agent of that which you serve."

Eric raised an eyebrow, genuinely perplexed. "What? What're you talking about?"

The man gave a slight laugh, stuffing his hands in his pockets as he leaned against the tree they had been using for shade. "The Darkness. You are its servant. Errand-boy. Sacrificial lamb. Whatever you want to call it." He raised his hand to stop Eric from speaking. "And before you go into an indignant tirade about how you're so great and moral and that no one controls your life, about how your humanity will triumph and evil will be vanquished, spare me. You *do* work for it, the same as me. Just because the horse thinks its job is simply to not get whipped doesn't mean it doesn't tote the plow just the same." He paused, giving a shrug before settling in to watch Eric.

Eric looked at Lindsay with concern. For now she was remaining silent, as if she understood that this was necessary. But he would have to explain all of this later. If there *was* a later. For there to be a chance, he needed to get her away from them.

"Why don't we go somewhere and talk?"

Mr. Teneber shook his head. "No, I don't think that would do. There isn't much time, and besides, this involves Lindsay as well." The little man gave her an ingratiating smile before turning his dark eyes back to Eric.

Eric clenched his teeth at her name. He needed to end this quickly. He wondered if he could call up the power he had used before if he needed it badly enough. "What do you want?"

"Want? Why to keep you alive, of course."

"Alive? I thought you all wanted to kill me to bring this big evil over into the world. What happened to that?"

Teneber continued to look at him, his expression unchanging. "Oh, we will kill you, but not yet. As Raziel told you, there is a time and a place for such things. We prefer to stick to the plan. To that end, I'm trying to keep you out of danger."

"What kind of danger exactly?"

"There's all kinds of dangers, naturally. Especially for one such as yourself. You'll find you draw quite a few nasty things out of the shadows. But I did have a more specific danger in mind. It seems that your would-be bodyguard has finally fought himself free from the little hole you left him in. I have it on very good authority that he hates you substantially more now than he did beforehand, and to be fair, he already truly loathed you."

Eric rose slowly to his feet, standing half a foot taller than the man and careful to keep himself between Teneber and Lindsay. "Why should I believe any of this?"

"Aside from the fact that I clearly know too much about what's going on to be some random lunatic? I suppose you're right. That's not much to go on. How about this?"

It took several seconds for Eric to realize that everything had fallen dead silent. He feared for an insane instant that he had been struck deaf, but then he heard the wind against his ears. Looking around, he saw why it was so quiet. Everything was frozen. People talking or in mid-step, a duck hanging in the air two feet above where it had been about to land in the cool, green water of the pond. The day hung in a moment in time, the world *stopped* for as far as he could see.

Eric's eyes grew wide, but when his gaze returned to Mr. Teneber, the little man looked bored. He took a step towards Teneber. "This is a trick. What did you do?"

"I froze everything. To avoid having an insipid and pointless conversation which we seem to be having anyway." He shrugged again. "But maybe it's still worth it if it proves a point."

"What point is that?"

Mr. Teneber smiled at him. "That I have the power to kill you easily if I wanted to. But I want you alive for now. And if you want the same, you should listen to me."

"I see. And..."

The man looked up at him and raised his hand. "I said listen. Starting now."

Eric nodded, anger dancing with fear in his stomach.

"Good. Now, you may be wondering a couple of things. The first of which being that if Raziel is working for me, then why is he any more of a danger than he was before? The simple truth is that before Deritus he valued his own survival more than revenge. That balance has now shifted." The small man chuckled, genuine warmth flickering across his face as his eyes momentarily grew distant. "He also used to harbor a small, secret hope that he could be redeemed. With your help he's managed to dispense with that illusion as well." The man's snapped his gaze back to Eric and continued on. "You're also no doubt wondering, as foolish as it is, if you can somehow kill me with whatever meager power you think you possess. No, you can't. You lack the power and control to even touch me."

Eric shifted uncomfortably at Teneber's accuracy. He looked over at Lindsay and saw she was unfrozen as well, still listening silently. Her lip was trembling now and her eyes looked slightly wild. He had to get her out of here now. He considered just telling her to run, trusting that Teneber would stay near him, but he couldn't risk it. She'd die if he did something rash, and after seeing what this man was capable of, he knew it wouldn't work anyway.

"And before you go through some pointless process of trying to convince your lady friend to stay behind or go into hiding, don't bother. You are close to this girl. Very close. Raziel will smell you on her a week from now or even a year. And when he finds her he will kill her."

Eric clenched his teeth and took two steps towards Teneber. "*Why?* Why would he do that? Why is any of this happening? WHY?"

Mr. Teneber smiled thinly, his pale lips stretching tight over his teeth. "Too many questions, most of which are utterly pointless. But as to why he'd kill the girl, that would be for the simple reason that he is planning on killing everyone that is close to you."

"But..."

The man waved his hand as if to ward off his next question. "He's already at work on it. That's the only reason he isn't closer to finding you right now. He's been busy killing your father. Finished about fifteen minutes ago."

Eric slammed the man against the tree, gripping fistfuls of his jacket in his hands as he pulled him back and ran him into the tree trunk again. "You *bastard*! I'm sick of this. Of all of this! Why don't I just kill *you*?"

The man smiled at him. "While I have every confidence that you'll wind up carrying Lindsay with you, would you prefer it if she were permanently blind for your little roadtrip? It might make the trip more interesting, but it would also slow you down."

Threads of ice crawled quickly through his veins as the air went out of him. The man could and would make good on any threat he made. He couldn't afford to doubt that. He stepped back and sighed, wiping his eyes with the back of his hand. "What do you want me to do?"

The man smoothed his jacket lapels and shrugged again. "I don't really care. But I don't have control over Raziel any longer, so I'd make my main focus staying away from him. And keeping her with you and safe. If he does find the pair of you, I doubt anything will save her, but you would certainly be her best chance."

Eric looked at Lindsay again, and to his surprise, she no longer looked awed or frightened. Instead, her face was contorted with fury as she silently watched the man before them. She cut her eyes towards him when he looked back, and her face softened for a moment as she gave his leg a squeeze from where she sat. He was turning away when he heard her speak.

"How long do we have?"

Mr. Teneber looked down at her, his eyes dark and murky. "Raziel is quite the speedy fellow. And unfortunately for you, he already knows you two are staying together. He's going to be at Lindsay's apartment in another eight minutes or so. After that, it won't take him too long to track you two down."

Eric wanted to keep Lindsay out of this as much as possible. Teneber giving her even the barest of glances sent a wave of fear through him so strong that he thought he'd be sick. He wanted the man to forget that she even existed. It was a foolish hope, but he had few left these days.

"If you're so powerful, why don't you just stop Raziel?"

"That's not my role in this."

Eric grimaced. "Whatever. Can we go now? According to you, time is wasting."

Mr. Teneber licked his lips and nodded. "Certainly, certainly. Have a good trip." He moved as if he was going to go, but then he turned back. "Oh, and don't worry about missing your date with destiny. I'll find you when the time is right. Til then." Without waiting for any response, he tipped his hat and began to crumble before their eyes, as if his entire body were made up of ash or tiny bits of newspaper. Within a matter of seconds the wind had carried it all away.

Eric looked around and saw that everything was moving and back to normal again. He felt some relief at that, but it was greatly overshadowed by his fear that Raziel would arrive any moment. Hearing a gasping sound, he turned to see Lindsay fighting for her breath, tears streaming down her cheeks. Sitting down next to her, he took her in his arms and stroked her hair, murmuring words he hoped were comforting. Before he realized it, he was simply saying that he was sorry over and over again.

She looked up at him then, her eyes fierce. "Don't ever apologize for yourself again. I have no fucking clue what's going on, but I know enough to know it isn't your fault."

He shook his head. "You can't know that. I don't even know that."

"Well I do. Now let's go." She stood and pulled him up as well.

He pulled her back to him, keeping hold of her hand as he spoke. "Lindsay, I don't know. He could be lying. I don't know how safe it will be with me."

She took him by the arm and made him start walking. "Maybe it is all a lie. But I don't think so, and neither do you. Either way, you're taking me with you. Now get moving. There's a bus station not too far from here."

They moved quickly through the park, leaving Lindsay's car where it sat, not wanting it left at the bus station as evidence of where they had gone. They walked silently and cautiously, their eyes darting in every direction as they watched for some sign of danger.

They couldn't be blamed for not noticing the two men that had kept them under surveillance since they had left Lindsay's apartment that morning. They were professionals, after all, and were paid well for their ability to go unnoticed. One of the men was sitting casually on a bench nearby while the second was sitting in a car at the edge of the park, casually concealing the parabolic ear that he had been using. As the couple walked away, he pulled a set of earphones out of his ears to replace them with a cell phone. A moment later the man on the bench answered his own phone.

The man in the car watched the pair walking off and snorted. He wondered if they were stoned. Their conversation had been very strange and had randomly jumped from one topic to another at one point near the end. It didn't matter. He had a feeling not much was going to matter for these two for much longer.

When he heard his partner answer his cell phone he kept his message short. "Tell Mr. Hobbes they're on the move."

Chapter Fourteen

This was the fourth witch that he had killed in a month. While Lawrence suspected that he was being more than a little overcautious, he was unwilling to take any chances. The first dream had come just over five weeks ago, and he had woken from it in sheets soaked in his own sweat and blood. He had thought he was dying at first, but then he realized that he only had a severe nosebleed.

But the dream had felt like dying, hadn't it? He could never remember the details on his own, but he could still sense certain things about them, and what he had discerned had filled him with fear and hopelessness at first. There was no question that they were more than simple dreams, and for days he was tormented by his inability to understand what they meant. But then he had begun seeking out some way of learning more about them, and that had led him to the witches.

For not the first time Lawrence considered the benefits of being rich and powerful. It had taken less than a week from when he had the first dream to locate and contact several members of a loosely-organized and world-spanning coven that claimed to be able to help him. He had kept his expectations very low, even though the ones he arranged appointments with all claimed to have special talent in what they called 'scrying dreams'. Bullshit, he had thought.

But he had been pleasantly surprised. The set-up had been similar each time. He would come into a room smelling faintly of pot and incense, lay down on a couch or bed of pillows, and focus on the dream. Then around five to ten minutes later the witch would begin to scream at the top of her lungs.

The first time it had come as quite a surprise. Lawrence had sat up quickly, pulling himself several feet further away from the woman that lay wailing and writhing on the floor nearby. To her credit, she had managed a span of marginal coherence for half an hour or so.

It was during this brief time that Lawrence had learned of the boy. Even now the mere thought of that moment of revelation caused anger to well up inside of him. After all of his years of work and dedication, some child was attempting to take his rightful place. Planning on usurping the destiny that was rightfully his. That *had* been his.

After that he was like a madman, pouring everything he had into finding this boy. But it was too large a task, even with his resources. In the end, he'd had to hope for another dream, and the wait had been a short one.

The second witch had suffered a catastrophic stroke while touching his dreams, and it was almost a mercy killing when he had his men take care of her. But the third had given him a diner in Kansas City, and within twelve hours he had the usurper under surveillance.

He would bide his time for now. He knew the dreams would keep coming. They were gifts and visions from his god, who wanted him to stop this foul boy who was trying to take his place. Waiting and watching, he would receive a sign when it was time to put his plan into action. Until then, he would just keep gathering the pieces.

Looking over at the dead woman sitting on the nearby ratty sofa he marveled again at the speed in which she had bitten out her own wrist. She likely would have bled to death anyway, but Lawrence would take no chance that any one of these freakshow whores could live to piece together anything substantial about the power he was striving to regain. He was too close to make a stupid mistake now.

And while this woman had crumbled fairly quickly, it wasn't as if she was useless. He had learned after the last witch to bring maps in case they needed them, and sure enough, this woman had began screaming for a map like a lunatic only a minute or two after they had begun. When handed the large U.S. Atlas they had brought along, Lawrence felt a moment of fear that she would need a map for somewhere other than America and that everything would end here in failure.

But the woman had flipped through the book enthusiastically, her eyes wild and foam trickling through her bared teeth as she fanned through the pages of borders and roads three times before finding what she wanted. Clearly satisfied by her discovery, she had murmured to herself before raising her arm to bite out a substantial chunk of her wrist.

Blood had begun spraying her face immediately, but she paid it no heed. She had simply run her other hand through the wound and calmly traced out a word across the map of Texas she had found. She had studied her handiwork for a moment before vomiting on herself and passing out.

Lawrence examined the map again, now photographed and safely sealed in a protective bag. His people said that on a first glance there appeared to be no significance to what was written aside from the obvious, with the handwriting style, word position, and the use of blood all having no special meaning in their opinion.

Still, overall Lawrence was very pleased with today's progress. Holding the map before him, he felt certain that this was the next big piece in the puzzle. The next step to the regaining of his destiny. He read the word aloud with some reverence--if not for what it meant to him now, for what it may represent in the future.

"Cave."

Chapter Fifteen

Riding on a bus in the middle of the night is an intimate experience. The lights are turned off aside from dim running lights along the aisle, and the air is thick and scarce. On a full bus, the feeling is something like what a cow must experience traveling with its brethren from home to home or from field to slaughter. The dark is filled with the occasional sounds of those around you. Sniffs and coughs, a laugh or light snoring. Constant reminders of the humanity that crowds around you, terrible and wonderful at the same time.

Eric sat awake through the first bus which took them to Mt. Vernon, but it was after eleven before they made the bus that would take them to Chicago, and the day's adventures had taken their toll. He was asleep before they had pulled out of the station.

When he awoke, his watch told him it was a few minutes after midnight. He felt a stab of guilt and he pulled back from Lindsay's shoulder where his head had been resting a moment before. She gave him a smile he could just make out in the dark.

"Did you have a good nap?"

He swallowed. "I'm sorry...I shouldn't have fallen asleep."

Raising her eyebrow, she shifted slightly to face him more. "Why not? You were tired. I slept on the last bus."

"But I got us into this. It's up to me to keep watch." He paused, fighting against his urge to go on and losing. "I'm sorry, Lindsay. I know I said it before, but I'm sorry."

He watched her eyes narrow. "Listen up. I'm tired of you apologizing for something that isn't your fault. Whatever all this is...Look, it's a mess, right? I don't know what's going on and I know that. If it wasn't you I wouldn't believe any of it. But it is and I do. And you're not to blame for it. You're the victim here."

"No, you are. Because of me."

He sucked in a breath when she slapped him across the face. "I'm not kidding. Shut up with the guilt-trip. Like I said, it's a mess. But it's *our* mess, and we'll deal with it."

Eric rubbed his cheek and shook his head slowly. "Why?"

She shrugged and sat back in her seat, putting a hand on his leg and giving it a squeeze. "Because I've seen a lot of bad in my life. Enough to know good when it walks through the door. And enough to hold on to it when it does."

Eric's initial plan had been to head to Georgia as quickly as possible to check on his father. It was Lindsay that had suggested calling home first and checking to see what the situation was before deciding what to do. He felt a moment of panic and shame when he had to struggle to remember his father's number, his hand trembling as he dialed the number for the automated collect call service.

The silence that followed seemed to stretch out forever, and he was on the verge of hanging up when he heard the mechanistic woman's voice say "Your call is connected." He felt his heart bloom with hope and relief. Then he realized the voice on the other end of the line was not his father's.

"Hello? Is this really Eric?" A woman's voice. Older.

"Yes? Who is this?"

"This is Mrs. Hammett. From down the street?"

"Uh, yeah. Mrs. Hammett. How are you? Um, is something wrong?"

A pause. "Honey, your father has passed away. I'm so sorry."

The cement block wall before him seemed to ripple as he swayed on his feet. He placed his palm against the smooth painted stone and blinked back tears. "Dead? You're sure?"

The woman let out a nervous laugh before responding. "Well, yes. I'm just over here tidying up now that the police...um, where are you, Honey?"

"Police? What about the police?"

"Eric, your father was murdered. Just a few hours ago. He was getting out of his car and somebody got him. It...It was terrible. They haven't found out who yet."

"Ah...ah....What about Grandpa? Is he okay?"

Another pause. "Shug, your grandfather died two years ago. Heart failure. You didn't know?"

The tears were trickling down his face now. "Um, no ma'am. I didn't."

"Well, the funeral will be on Tuesday. Everything's taken..." He hung up, resting his head against the pay phone. He jumped when Lindsay's hand touched his back. He turned around, not thinking to wipe his eyes.

"They're gone. My father...and grandfather. They're gone."

To his surprise, her eyes were shining with tears as well. "*Oh, I'm sorry.*" She put her arms around him, stroking the back of his head. She had to stand on tiptoes as he buried his face into her shoulder, crying softly. Cursing himself.

Finally she pulled herself away and looked up at him with a watery smile. "I've always wanted to see Wisconsin. How about you?"

Before he knew it, before he thought, he was kissing her. There was an instant where she seemed to draw back in surprise, but then she was against him, kissing him back softly. He felt his body responding already, his heart speeding as he felt the kiss deepen. It seemed to take every ounce of his willpower to finally pull back, giving her a grin that made her laugh.

"That's a good smile."

He wiped his eyes and looked away for a moment. "Yeah, yeah. Wisconsin sounds good." When he looked back down at her she was still smiling, her eyes bright. He gave her another quick kiss and pulled her along, his face serious again. "We better get going."

There was a time, soon after Eric realized the visions he had of others' lives were more than vivid daydreams, that he strongly considered the possibility that he was crazy. Back then, he had thought about checking himself in somewhere or even going back to his father for help. But whenever he was close to doing either, he would talk himself out of it, putting off making a final decision. In time he came to realize that there was truth to what he saw, as terrible as it was. When he managed to reconcile himself to that truth, he began to accept the visions as a part of his life.

They were sporadic, and he could go for days or even weeks without having the slightest twinge. Aside from when he first met Lindsay and a handful of other times, he could see no reason for why he saw what he did, and he came to look at it as something he would never fully understand.

Then came Raziel, and he had his explanation. In the weeks that had followed, he had looked at the flashes that came to him with new eyes, and a shadow had stolen over his heart every time he was overtaken by images of some dark deed or thought occurring or soon to pass. After he escaped Deritus, he rarely thought of the visions at all, and when he did it was only with relief that they hadn't returned since he had summoned the black storm that had protected him in the library.

They were still an hour out of Chicago when the flashes came back. The flood of images came as a surprise, taking his breath away as dozens of sights, smells, and sensations filled his brain. The woman sitting in front of them was cheating on her husband and was worried because her period was late and she was *never* late. The man sitting across the aisle from Lindsay was going to die in his tub in less than a week. The couple two rows behind them were going to be crippled in a car crash three years from now. The bus driver was thinking about how he had killed his best friend two nights ago and *no one knew.*

Eric felt his gorge rise, slamming his head into the luggage rack overhead as he leapt out of his seat and climbed swiftly over a startled Lindsay to race back to the cramped and dingy lavatory. He splashed water on his face, air coming in short gasps. When Lindsay knocked on the door a few seconds later, he sent her away. His senses were still overwhelmed by the deluge of misfortune and evil deeds, and he realized he was hyperventilating. Closing his eyes, he forced himself to calm down, not fighting the images but instead focusing on creating a still center in the eye of the storm. His mind cast about for a serene image, a thing of peace or joy that he could use to anchor himself. He smiled slightly when he settled on Lindsay. He thought of her and slowly expanded the peace that the thought brought him, pushing the dark flashes into the background. Several times he faltered, thoughts of her growing sick invading the increasing stillness within him. But fighting those thoughts, he continued to work until the visions were on the periphery of his senses. Soon they had faded away altogether, the crushing blackness passing with them.

It was still a few minutes before he could trust himself to leave the bathroom, and when he returned to his seat, the concern was plain on Lindsay's face.

"Are you okay?" She touched his arm and frowned at him. "Was it something you ate?"

Giving her a shaky smile he shook his head. "No, I don't think so. I'm okay now. But when we get to Chicago, if we have time I'd like to talk about some stuff. You deserve a lot of explanations and I've got a lot to tell you."

Her expression was strange as she nodded. "Yeah, okay. Sounds good. When we get to Chicago."

Eric settled back into his seat, trying to get comfortable and wanting to get back to sleep for a little while before they reached the bus stop. Instead he found himself thinking about what he would tell Lindsay, searching for words in the dark.

They sat across from each other in molded plastic chairs of rainbow colors. The colors may have once been intended to raise the spirits of those that frequented the Chicago bus stop, but age and poor lighting had taken away any former charm. The bus stop was huge and extremely busy, even this early in the morning, but after some effort they had managed to find this secluded terminal away from all the noise--and to be fair, smells--that permeated the rest of the station. Eric wanted to do this right.

"Now that we're here I don't know how to start."

Lindsay shrugged. He thought she looked nervous and he could sympathize given the flips his own stomach were doing. "Start wherever you want. The beginning is always good."

"Um. I just...Okay. When I was in fourth grade I got into a fight."

He told her everything, or at least everything that he could think of that might be related to what was happening to them. He told her about seeing Raziel for the first time and then again when he began his road trip with the fallen angel. He told her about the night his mother died, and how five other people had died simultaneously within minutes of him finding out. He told her about Deritus and about how he had saved her from Ralph Tuggle. He told her about seeing her father die.

She asked only a few questions throughout, her face showing a myriad of emotions as she took every detail in. He realized after it was too late that he had ended his story with the bank robbery, saving it for the last because he hating having to tell her. Now he wished he had found some better way to do it—something more artful that would take away the hurt look that had come into her eyes.

"So...um. Well, I think that's everything." He looked down at his watch and saw they had forty minutes until their bus.

"Hmm. Yeah. You know how crazy all of this sounds, right?"

He nodded, not looking up.

"I mean, the whole thing is like some kind of religious psycho delusion."

He looked up, his temper flaring slightly. "Look, I get it. If you don't believe me, fine."

Lindsay's eyes widened in surprise. "I didn't say that! I do. I believe all of it. When that guy met us in the park..."

He sat back in his chair. "Well yeah, the strange man freezing everything does kind of give my story some credibility."

She frowned at him. "Don't be an ass. What I was going to say is that when we ran into that guy, yeah, that clued me in. But even without any of that, I would believe you."

"Why? *I* wouldn't believe me. It sounds fucking insane."

She sighed, her face suddenly sad. "I need to tell you something. Something bad. Well, bad in a way at least."

He felt a weight settle into his stomach. What more could there be? "Okay. What is it?"

She laced her hands under her knees as she leaned forward, her face pale as she held his gaze and paused a moment as if thinking how to best begin. Finally, she plunged in.

"Eric, I don't have cancer."

"Um what?"

"I....I lied." The first tear trickled down from the corner of her eye. "I... can explain. I just..."

He swept her up in a hug that nearly knocked the breath from her in a startled gasp. He started kissing her face, grinning and laughing as he pulled back to look at her. "You're okay? Really? No joke?"

"I'm okay. Really. But listen. I need to tell you why."

"If you're okay it doesn't matter. I don't care." He started kissing her again, but she pushed him back.

"No. It does matter. I need to tell you."

He nodded and sat down beside her, still grinning. She turned to face him, a slight smile on her face, tears still fresh in her eyes. "I...When you passed out in the diner, I didn't know anything about you. I just knew you were this guy that had saved me years before. That meant a lot. But still, you were a stranger.

"But watching over you as you slept, I started thinking that you looked like a good person. Someone that would be good to know. Then when you woke up, I felt this instant...I don't want to say attraction because it wasn't sexual. Uh, not that I didn't find you attractive in that way, because I did, but..."

Eric laughed softly and nodded. "I know what you mean. Go on."

"Well, I was just *drawn* to you. And the thought of you leaving without my getting to know you scared me. A lot. I don't know why. And when you told me about Raziel, I knew you'd leave fast if you thought I was in danger. So it was all I could come up with."

"Okay. That makes sense."

"I would have told you before now, I wanted to, but I kept being afraid you'd leave if you found out. That you'd be mad at me or that you'd be afraid of me getting hurt."

Eric nodded. "I get it. Really. But why would I be mad? Do you know how much I've worried about this? About whether I should leave or not, and what would happen to you if I did? Worrying that I was falling for somebody that would leave me so soon? This is the best news I've ever had."

She looked unsure. "Really?"

"Yes, really." He grinned and stood up. "My God, think about my life. It's not exactly normal or the most upbeat story you'd ever want to hear. You lying about *not* actually dying is not really going to register as a big trauma in my book. Quite the opposite."

"So you're really okay with this?"

He pulled her to her feet. "Can you deal with all my drama?"

She frowned at him. "Yeah, of course."

"Then I think I can overlook this. Now we better go before we miss our bus." He started walking and turned back to find Lindsay staring at him. "What's the matter?"

"You're very strange, you know."

He walked back to her, grinning. "You lie about having terminal diseases. People in glass houses." Giving her a kiss, he put his arm around her waist. "Come on. Clock's a ticking."

Chapter Sixteen

"It's a sign. Or a trap. Maybe it's a sign that it's a trap."

Lindsay poked him in the side, laughing against his neck as she whispered to him. "It'll be fine. Buses break down all the time. And this bus has got to be twenty years old if it's a day."

He stood up, peering out the windows before stepping out into the aisle with a shake of his head. "I don't know. I guess. We've just got to be careful."

"We will be. And this'll give us a chance to stretch our legs. I was about to get a permanent cramp sitting there."

They stepped off the bus into the noonday sun, the brilliant blue of the sky carrying an edge of unreality after the last few hours of dreary travel. The bus had limped along to the edge of a service station on the fringes of a small town called Lewiston. According to the bus driver, they were less than fifteen miles from the Wisconsin border.

They had passed through the town already, and while there wasn't much to it, what there was seemed nice enough. Taking in a deep breath of cool air, Eric shaded his eyes with his hand and looked around.

"Well, the driver said we're going to be ready to roll in an hour and a half. What do you want to do til then?"

Lindsay shrugged. "I dunno. I don't think we should wander too far in case they get done quicker than they say. We passed a house just up the road that was having an estate sale. We could go wander around there for a little while just to kill time."

He paused before nodding. "Yeah, I guess so. Lead the way."

The interior of the house had a stale, unused smell that seemed strange to Eric given that the house had presumably been lived in up until very recently. They walked in through a side door that was propped open, the gloom of the shadowy rooms within settling around his heart as they walked further inside. He hated the idea of estate sales, hated the idea of being in someone's house uninvited, knowing that the last memories formed there were of death and loss.

Seeing random items scattered throughout the living room they were in, he noticed small price stickers stuck to them. Moving over to a bookshelf, he plucked a book down and opened it, finding what he first thought was a paper bookmark inside. Looking at the paper closer, he realized it was an English essay, written a number of years before, the edges of the composition notebook paper yellowed and curled. Underneath a boy's name was '7th Grade'. He had gotten a 'B' on the paper.

He felt like a ghoul being here, picking over the remains of the lives that had been lived here. Gently placing the book back on the shelf, he left Lindsay looking at stacks of old magazines and wandered into a hallway which led to the kitchen.

He couldn't fully get away from his feeling of unease, and the fact that they hadn't seen anybody was only making it worse. Who left a house open and unattended? Didn't they worry about being robbed blind? He entered the kitchen and saw that the counters were covered with appliances and dishes, silverware and kitchen knives. All priced and ready to sell. He was about to go back to Lindsay when he realized someone was sitting at the kitchen table at the far end of the room.

The old woman was small and gray, her eyes faded but still quick as she read through the newspaper in front of her. He felt relief at seeing someone finally, and was momentarily cheered at her alertness and apparent sharpness given her age. Then he noticed the stack of newspapers that sat beside her on the table and realized that she was likely reading one of many pages of random paper gathered to wrap dishes that were sold.

Still, she was probably just bored and wanted something to do. He felt sorry for her, wondering if it was her husband that had died. He thought about leaving her alone, but decided against it. It'd be rude to not at least say hello.

"Come on and sit down for a bit. You're the first person to come by in over an hour."

He jumped slightly in surprise at her words, and then did as he was bade, smiling as he walked up to the table and sat down.

"Hey there. I'm Eric. My girlfriend and I were just looking around while our bus gets fixed down the road."

The woman's eyes jumped to his own, intense and bright now that they were upon him. "I see. Well I'm glad you stopped by. My sister is running this thing, but she ran to get us lunch. Found anything you like?" She shifted in her seat, neatening the stack of newspapers beside her before looking back at him.

"Well, we're just passing through and browsing really." He paused before adding, "You've sure got a lot of nice stuff though."

The old woman raised her hand and waved away his compliment. "Not my stuff. My daughter's. And most of it's overpriced junk. But it was dear to her, I suppose."

He frowned, unsure what to say but feeling that he needed to respond. Finally he asked the most obvious question. "Was your daughter the one who passed?"

She nodded matter-of-factly. "Yes, she died two weeks ago. My son-in-law's moving back to Florida with my grandchildren tomorrow, and I'll be going to live with my sister in Chicago. What did you say your name was?"

"Eric."

The woman laughed harshly. "Where're your manners, Eric? What's your full name?"

"Oh, sorry. Eric Talbot, ma'am. What's yours?"

The woman looked out the window for a moment. "Yes, Chicago. It's a dirty city, but I don't suppose I have a choice, do I?"

He stayed silent, wondering if he should answer.

She touched the newspaper stack again, slowly pulling out a snub-nosed revolver from between the pages. "My name is Louisa Stalling, Eric. I've been waiting for you a long, long time."

Eric jerked in his chair, but managed to fight his urge to stand up or reach for the gun. It was already pointed at him, and he was liable to get shot if he made any quick moves. At this distance she would have to work to *not* hit him.

"What...What do you mean, Mrs. Stalling?"

She looked at him strangely. "You don't know?"

"No ma'am. I've never seen you before in my life."

Her hand began to tremble under the weight of the gun, so she rested the butt of the gun on the table to steady it. "No, maybe you don't. Ah well."

"Ma'am, can you point that away from me please? I don't mean you any harm. I think this is all a big mistake."

Louisa smiled at him sadly and shook her head. "No mistake. I've got the letter, and I know what the dream told me."

God, she's totally insane. What if Lindsay comes in and...I've got to get the gun away from...

"You look so confused though. It's strange. But I have to do it. I have to."

"Do what?"

She nodded to herself, only her constant glances up letting him know that she still knew he was there. "Maybe if I explain it'll help make it easier."

"Yeah, help me understand."

"It started with the letter. The letter that Rupert's war buddy brought to me." Her eyes grew distant as she began remembering. "I had gotten the letter about Rupert's suicide while he was stationed in Germany a few months before. But it was one of the soldiers under him that brought me Rupert's Purple Heart and the second letter." She tapped her lips with one withered finger as she frowned in thought. "What was that fellow's name? Harry or something like that. His last name was Chambry, that much I remember.

"Anyway, he gave me the medal in a nice little wooden box and then handed me this letter. It was all crumpled in a dirty envelope, but the way he handed it to me you would think it was the most important thing in the world. He left soon after and I opened it as soon as he was out of sight. It was strange to say the least. The page was blank except for a single name, and that wasn't even written in my Rupert's hand. The name was Eric Talbot."

What is this? What's going on? How much time until Lindsay comes looking for me? He glanced at the door behind the woman and saw nothing, and he had heard no sign of Lindsay approaching from behind him. Yet. *I've got to find some way to distract this crazy bitch so I can get the gun.*

The woman paused to let this sink in before continuing. "Of course I had no idea what it was all about, and I had no way of contacting this Chambry fellow, so I just put the letter in a shoebox and didn't think much of it over the years.

"Then two weeks ago, the same night that my daughter Jessica died at the hospital, I had a dream. In the dream, Rupert came to me, just as handsome as he had ever been. But he was crying. He was telling me how sorry he was for leaving me all those years ago...that it had all been a terrible mistake. That because he had killed himself he was condemned to Hell. That he couldn't be with me when I went to Heaven. I screamed and cried in the dream...I never loved anything like I loved my Rupert...and he hugged me and told me how sorry he was.

"I asked wasn't there any way we could be together, and he said there *was* a way, but it was dangerous. I didn't care. He told me that I would run across a man. A man that would look like a nice, decent young man. But that this man would be the cause of great evil in the world. Unless he was stopped.

"I knew what he wanted, and it scared me, but I was willing to be brave for his sake. I asked who this man was, but that's when I woke up."

Louisa coughed into her hand, and for a moment the gun lowered half an inch, but then it passed and her eyes were on him again. "When I woke up, I was sitting on my bedroom floor with papers all around me. Apparently I had been rummaging in my closet while I was asleep. And in my hand was the letter with the name on it. Your name."

Eric felt icy dread creeping over him, the shadow of inevitability deepening the dark corners of the room. "Listen, this is a big mistake. You're being tricked. We both are."

She smiled at him again, the sadness growing in her features. "I've prayed about this and thought about it. I don't see any other way. Rupert wouldn't lie to me, and it can't just be a dream or my imagination, can it? You're here in front of me, after all." She seemed to be talking more to herself than to him. "I...I have to do it. My sister will be back soon. I have to do it now." She raised her gun, the barrel dancing in her wavering grip. "I'm so sorry."

I've got to grab it no...

Lindsay moved in a blur, darting through the doorway behind the woman. She was at the counter and then at Louisa's side in one fluid movement. When she stopped, she had a steak knife jabbed into the side of the old woman's neck, dimpling the wrinkled flesh the blade found there.

"Put down the gun or I'll kill you." Lindsay's voice was cold and hard, her face tight as she spoke the words.

The woman's eyes widened in fear and Eric felt a moment of sympathy for her. Tears began to well from the corners of her eyes. "I can't...I have to do it. Even if you kill me. For Rupert."

Lindsay's expression didn't change. "I won't stop with you. I'll kill your sister when she comes back too. Don't fucking think I won't."

"No!...Why?" The woman's chin quivered.

"Why not? You take away somebody I love, why shouldn't I do the same?"

"No...I..." Louisa's face was the picture of torment for a moment, and then she broke. Dropping the gun to the table, she put her face in her hands and began sobbing softly.

Lindsay looked at him now. She mouthed "let's go" as she slipped the knife into her jacket pocket and stepped back to the doorway. He nodded and stood quietly, picking up the gun and emptying it before putting it on top of the refrigerator. He almost stopped to say something comforting, but realized the uselessness of anything he might offer.

Thinking better of it, he followed Lindsay out of the house, leaving the woman to her grief.

Lindsay kept kissing and hugging him, even after they were back on the bus and rolling down the road.

"Are you sure you're okay?" She was looking at him nervously again as if she was afraid he might keel over at any given moment.

He gave her a smile he didn't really feel and nodded. "I'm fine. Everything's okay."

"I thought I was going to lose you. I thought..." She fell silent and hugged him again, burying her face in his shoulder. They rode on in silence for some time before easing back into conversation--idle chatter to avoid talking about what had happened, at least for now. Yet as the miles ticked by Eric found he could think of little else.

When they reached Madison they checked into the cheapest room they could find at a hotel on the city square, the state capital visible from across the road. When Lindsay asked for a king bed, he tried to not show any surprise.

It was a few minutes after eight when they got into the room, both of them tired and hungry. The room was dark and had a chill about it, but was nice enough once they turned on a few lights. Lindsay went to the bathroom and Eric sat on the edge of the bed, idly flipping through channels as he thought about Louisa Stalling and what his encounter with her might signify.

"What's the matter?"

He looked up to find Lindsay looking at him with concern. Shrugging, he leaned forward, his elbows propped on his knees as he looked at the television again, the volume muted. "How much did you hear of what that woman was telling me today?"

She came and sat down beside him. "The first thing I heard was her talking about some soldier that her husband fought with came to visit her. I almost walked in then, but then I noticed the gun."

He nodded, still not looking up. "That guy, the one that visited her? I'm pretty sure that was my grandfather."

Eric saw her jerk in surprise out of the corner of his eye. "What? You're kidding."

"It would be my mother's father, and he died a few months after I was born, but that was his name. I know it had to be him. Nothing else makes any sense." He laughed bitterly. "Not that any of this does."

"Well, maybe..."

He turned and looked at her, his face falling. "I'm tired, Lindsay."

"Well, let's get some sleep. I could use some rest too."

Shaking his head, he stood up. "That's not what I mean. I mean I'm tired of all this...bullshit. Of being threatened and chased. Of being manipulated. Someone had to set all of this in motion *decades* ago, knowing that I was going to be in that house today. What kind of sense does that make? And why do it? To kill me? To trust killing me to a little old woman? What kind of sense does *that* make?" He began pacing. "I...You know, I don't really think today was about killing me. It was just about *pushing* me. Pushing me away from one thing or toward another. Manipulating me. And I'm *fucking sick of it.* All of it." He sat back down, slumping onto the bed.

"I don't know what to do."

She moved herself onto his lap, facing him. Cradling his face in her hands, she smiled, but her eyes were serious. "I don't either. But that's okay. Sometimes you aren't supposed to know. We just have to take things as they come."

"But..." She put two fingers on his mouth.

"We just have to take things as they come, and hope for the best. Trust that if we do our best things will turn out okay."

He nodded, sighing. She moved her fingers from his mouth and started kissing him. He kissed her back, feeling a charge race through him as the kiss deepened and she pressed herself against him. Falling back onto the bed, he savored the weight and warmth of her as he moved his hands under her shirt and across her soft, smooth skin.

Soon they were kissing each other everywhere, moving together, exploring one another. Slowly at first, savoring, and then faster as the tension stretched taut between them, binding them in a place outside of time and trouble. They were together, and for now that was all that mattered. For now, that was enough.

Chapter Seventeen

The wind sliced through Eric as he walked towards the capital square, impressed as always by the towering beauty of Madison's capital building. It had apparently been designed by Frank Lloyd Wright, and he had to admit that it put the Georgia capital to shame, even if the inside had a few more badgers decorating the doorways than he was strictly comfortable with.

They had been in Madison for nearly two weeks now, and while they had initially planned to move on much sooner, they had found a lot to like about the city. It was a very eclectic and artsy place, with a sense of life that cheered Eric in a way that few places had in the last few years. He enjoyed going into the variety of stores that the area around the capital provided--especially the bookstores. They had spent the better part of one morning roaming the dark shelves of one such store that had a basement level that seemed to stretch on and on, as if the owners had secretly tunneled under all the nearby shops to make room for more of their own wares.

In fact, the only real drawback he saw to the area was the cold. It was already late spring, and there had still been several days where the chill was bitter and harsh, at least from the perspective of a nice Southern boy. It didn't seem to bother Lindsay as much, so he didn't mention it to her, but that didn't keep his teeth from chattering. Up ahead he saw the restaurant they were meeting at and his pace quickened without thinking. He had been against their splitting up from the beginning, but Lindsay had finally convinced him that it was for the best. She said they couldn't live their lives in fear, and that they couldn't spend every single moment together anyway. If they were cautious, everything should be fine.

Sure.

He tried not to run.

Lindsay felt her heart speed up as Eric entered the restaurant, waving to him at the same time he spotted her. She spread the newspaper out before her and tried not to look nervous as he sat down.

"What's up? Did you have a good time?"

He nodded. "Yeah, it was fun. I saw the Orpheum is going to have live music tonight. Want to go?"

"Sure, what kind?"

Eric shrugged. "It didn't say. The name sounded kind of funky, so maybe jazz. Dunno." He grinned. "I haven't been able to keep up with all the hip music of late. What about you? Did the phone call with your mother go okay?"

She shifted in her chair. "Yeah, as well as could be expected." That wasn't a total lie she supposed. She had gotten an answer machine and left a vague message telling her mother she was alive and well. Given her typical conversations with her mother, that was about as well as *could* be expected.

Wanting to change the subject and anxious to bring it up anyway, she pushed the newspaper across to him, tapping the ad she had circled. "I wanted to show you something I ran across. Check that out."

He picked up the paper and studied it, his expression not changing as he raised his eyes to look at her again. "A farmhouse? For us to rent?"

She nodded slightly, trying to keep the enthusiasm out of her voice. "It's just a thought I had when I saw it. Staying at the hotel is getting pricey, even using my credit card. With this, I bet we could rent it by the week for a lot less. Just for a little while." She was starting to ramble and she knew it, but she couldn't stop from saying a little more. "It's just a thought. We don't have to look at it if you don't want to."

He reread the ad again before nodding. "It sounds great. I don't know how long we should stay here though. Not *here*, but anywhere." He paused and looked at her, his expression softening. "But I don't guess it'll hurt anything to just look it over. We'll need to get a rental car I guess. I don't know how far this is, but it has to be a decent piece if it's on a farm."

The house had been a bit rundown, and even with the approaching dusk to soften its rough edges, it was clear to both of them that it was not a very pretty house. Still, it was certainly secluded, which to Eric's mind was a big asset. He had decided that it was very unlikely that Raziel had much in the way of supernatural tracking abilities given his failure to track them down thus far. If that was the case, then laying low might be as good of a plan as moving around all the time. He felt a little hopeful buzz as they left the house, and he had dozed off before they were two miles down the long road back to the city.

He woke up as if from a nightmare, the weight of fear still heavy on his chest. He looked around, groggy from being pulled from deep sleep so quickly and more than a little disoriented. Lindsay was driving silently, not yet realizing that he had awoken. When he looked out he saw the blacktop rolling under them, highlighted by the headlights as they cut through the darkness. When he saw the figure suddenly appear in front of them, he only managed a slight choking sound before he heard the squeal of the brakes and felt the hammer blow of the car striking the thing that blocked their path.

The next few moments were chaos as the car's front end crumpled in where it struck the man, compressing into a V-shape even as the back of the car lifted five feet off the ground before slamming back down. Eric felt a line of fire across his chest where the safety belt had sliced into him, but otherwise he was fine. He looked over to find Lindsay peering wild-eyed at him from around the edge of the air bag that had deployed on her side.

"What...What did we just hit?"

He had only had a glimpse, but he knew. "Come on. We've got to get out of here. *Now.*"

She nodded and clawed at her seatbelt, getting it undone as he pulled her across the center console and out of the car with him, unwilling to let her out of his sight for even a moment. They were on their feet and turning to run when Raziel spoke.

"Hey Eric. Who's your little friend?"

He felt a wave of nausea roll through him as he turned, pulling Lindsay behind him. Raziel was standing less than ten feet away, his clothes ripped from the car's impact but otherwise unfazed. Steam rose in wisps from his body, whether from the impact or from the speed he had been moving before stopping in the road he couldn't say. Even in the dark Eric could see that the angel was smiling.

"Leave us alone. Just leave us the fuck alone."

Raziel gave a harsh, rasping laugh and he felt Lindsay tremble slightly against his back. Had Raziel been so *big* before? He supposed he had. He had to get Lindsay out of here.

"What do you want, Raziel?"

The angel laughed again, his voice cold. "You're very demanding for someone who abandoned me in that pit of hell to be eaten alive. Seems that I should be the one asking the questions and making the demands."

"Fine. You're the boss."

"There we go. That's a start. Now, as for what I want? I want the same thing I've always wanted. To keep you safe until I get to kill you with my bare hands."

"Go fuck yourself!" He felt Lindsay lunge against his back and he would have laughed if he weren't terrified. As it was, he was about to speak to cover for her when Raziel beat him to it.

"Such a nice little lady you have there. I think I'll have to twist her head off before we get going. How does that sound?"

Eric clenched his teeth. "I'll kill you if you get near her."

"Eric, you're such a useless, clueless turd. You can't stop me. You're about to piss your pants just standing there."

This wasn't far from the truth. From the moment of impact, Eric had known what was coming. And he had been afraid and angry, growing more so every second. And focusing every bit of that emotion until he needed to use it as a trigger. Now, without saying another word, he pulled that trigger.

Black energy engulfed him before arching away like midnight lightning, slamming into Raziel before he had any chance to dodge or even scream. Then the angel was gone, sent hurtling away with such force that when he struck the corner of the car it sheared off the metal cleanly, spinning the car around several times before it came to rest in the ditch. It's likely that the car would have struck and killed them if the force of Raziel striking it had not also propelled it forward just enough that the taillights swept less than a foot in front of Eric's midsection as it began its first rotation. Eric was already slumped on the ground by the second spin, gasping for breath as Lindsay tried to hold him up.

"I...I don't know if it'll stop him...get away...run..."

"I saw a place we can go a mile or two back. Come on." She started lifting him, grunting with the effort as he struggled to find his feet. After several attempts he managed to stand weakly, Lindsay supporting nearly the whole of his weight as they lurched forward together. At first he thought they were going to stay on the road, but he soon realized they were moving into the woods.

"Where are...where are we going?"

Lindsay puffed out a breath into his ear. "Shortcut. I think. I hope."

They stumbled on through scrub bushes and stands of hardwoods, and as the minutes crawled by Eric began to feel slightly better, his strength and balance returning slowly. Several times they would hear a noise and freeze where they stood, but nothing else would come and then they would travel on. He felt his feet beginning to go numb from the cold and wondered if they were lost. But just then they broke through the trees into a gravel parking lot, with Lindsay tugging at his arm as they raced toward the building ahead of them.

The church stood immense and solemn in the middle of the large parking lot, trees surrounding it on three sides and the road they had been traveling on winding along the fourth. As they drew closer he saw that it was a Catholic church, and Eric felt an insane moment of novelty as he realized he had never been in a Catholic church before. Now he was about to break into one.

As it happened, they didn't have to break in. The door was unlocked and they stepped into a dimly lit vestibule. Lindsay stood bent over, breathing heavily as he leaned against the closed door.

She looked up at him. "Are you feeling okay now?"

He nodded. "Not great, but better. At least it wasn't like at the diner."

Lindsay was about to respond when they heard a bellowing scream from outside.

"YOU CAN'T STAY IN THERE FOREVER! AND I'LL BE OUT HERE WHEN YOU COME OUT!"

Eric moved over to a window near the door and looked out. Raziel was outside, his left arm dangling uselessly at his side as he lurched back and forth a few feet from the front steps of the church. He turned to Lindsay, who had moved beside him to peer out as well.

"He can't come in here I don't think."

She smiled grimly. "That's what I was hoping. I didn't know if it would really work."

He put his arm around her, giving her a squeeze. "It was a great idea. You saved our necks."

She shrugged, looking out the window again. "I guess. For the moment at least."

"I'LL BE WAITING! I'LL BE WAITING!"

Eric pulled her away from the window and led her further into the church. "Let's see if anyone else is here, and then we can decide what to do next."

Chapter Eighteen

After exploring every room in the church, Eric had come to the conclusion that it was brand new and likely not even open yet. There was sawdust coating the floor in some places, and walls were unpainted in an entire hallway of rooms. He supposed that might explain why the front door was open at least.

If it was a work in progress, it wouldn't be for long. Most of the rooms were already fully furnished, and it wasn't long before they had found one of the daycare rooms and spread out sleep mats from the stack in the corner. Now they sat on them as they tried to figure out what to do next. They had no good ideas so far, and Eric only had one idea at all. After several minutes of silence while they pondered the situation, he decided to bring it up.

"Maybe I should just go out and let him take me."

Lindsay jerked her head up, staring at him. "What? Are you joking?"

He shook his head. "No, I'm serious. If I go out, he won't hang around here waiting for you to come out. You'll be safe." She started to protest but he raised his hand to stop her. "And then I'll get away from him again and meet you."

"There's no way. You can't guarantee he won't just kill you. Or that you'll be able to get away again."

"You saw what I did to him before."

She frowned slightly at that. She had yet to say anything about what she had seen him do. "Yeah, and he kept coming. He'd have caught us if we hadn't lucked up on this place. It's too big a risk. *Way* too big."

"But..."

"Besides, what if he *did* kill you? According to him, that'd let the Darkness into our world, right?"

Eric nodded, puffing out a discouraged breath. "Yeah, you're right. I know it. I just wish I could think of something."

She scooted closer to him, curling her arm through his own. "We'll come up with a way out. Don't worry." He kissed the top of her head, staring out into space as he tried to go back over their options. Deep in thought, it took him a moment to realize Lindsay was talking again.

"Eric, do you believe in God?"

He looked down at her with surprise. "Where did that come from?"

She shrugged. "Maybe it's the surroundings. But it's something I've thought about asking you before. Do you?"

He leaned away so he could look at her better. "Well, when I was growing up I never really knew what to think. My mama was always a firm believer, and Daddy never said anything about it much either way. I tend to think he just didn't think about it. As for me, it made sense enough that God would exist, especially considering some of the things that happened to me growing up. I just wasn't sure.

"Then when Mama died...Well, I told you what happened at the hospital. The people dying, my father not wanting anything else to do with me. All of that, I didn't understand it at the time, and I decided there couldn't be a God to let something that terrible happen, or if there were, that I didn't want any part of Him."

Lindsay took in what he was saying, sadness creeping into her features as he spoke. "And now?"

He sighed. "Well now...I don't guess I have a lot of choice but to believe in Him, do I? If I'm going to accept that this is all happening, that I've got a rogue angel and all these evil things after me, it kind of stands to reason that God's in the mix somehow. So yeah, I believe in God. I just don't trust Him."

"Why?"

"Well, let's look at the facts. Everyone that's ever meant anything to me is dead except for you, and you're being hunted down by the aforementioned fallen angel also wants me dead. I've spent years hiding and on the run now--from Raziel lately, and before that, from myself. And I don't see anything I've done to deserve any of it. That any of us have done to deserve it." Lindsay moved to respond, but he continued on.

"And aside from my own personal gripes, I've seen the evil that goes on in the world. My 'gift' has let me see way more of the bad things that happen to people than I ever wanted to. And it's getting to where now I can always feel the buzz of it in the background, like I could reach out and tap into a flood of hate and anger and misfortune anytime I liked. Because it's all the time. Because it's everywhere. If God is good and loves us so much, why let all those things happen? Why let Evil exist at all?"

Lindsay frowned at him. "That seems so...arrogant to me. Why does God let bad things happen to good people. Why not? What right do we have to ask God for anything, let alone some kind of guarantee that we'll never have a bad moment?

Eric's eyes widened at her vehemence. "Listen, I don't want to argue."

"We're not arguing. But this is important. Why should we have any kind of guarantee?"

"Because He made us. He made us and He screws with us. It's like buying a puppy and then spending half your time kicking it."

"It's not like that at all. God is God. The bad that happens is for a purpose, and it all balances out. But we have to trust in that, because we can't see every consequence of *anything* that happens. Even if it didn't balance out, that would be okay. Existing at all is such a gift. Anything beyond that is gravy."

"Gravy, huh? I don't know if a child that's homeless or a guy with terminal bone cancer would agree with you."

She shook her head. "They may not. Because they're in the moment and they're in pain. They're human and flawed. They're not God. That's what faith is about."

"Maybe. I don't know. But I still don't know why we need Evil at all. Even if it balances out, that doesn't explain why it's necessary in the first place."

"Because we need bad things to happen so we appreciate the good. And because we need to struggle to grow stronger. To me, it's the same reason that we have free will."

"Heh. Given the way I've been getting jerked around, I think that's debatable too."

She poked him in the chest with a finger. "You're still choosing your own path. That's why you're here with me instead of riding the roads with that lunatic outside. Right?"

"I guess."

"Right. One of the reasons I think we have evil and free will is so our lives will have meaning. So our choices will have significance. Because they're our own. If God just gave us everything good and nothing bad, if He didn't give us the ability to choose what we did and what we believed, none of it would be worth much, would it? And any love or belief we gave Him would have no real meaning.

"It's our struggle and our power to choose that makes us human and makes us matter. It's the fact that we choose to believe in God and love Him that gives that belief and love their worth and power."

Eric looked towards the window, the shadows of trees dimly visible in the yellow glare of a security light outside. "What about me? I didn't choose to have this evil thing put in me. I didn't choose any of this."

Lindsay leaned forward, taking his face in her hands, her eyes glimmering with unshed tears. "I know. I know you didn't." She paused for a moment, looking into his eyes before going on. "When I went into my apartment that day, Tuggle was too fast for me. He had the knife in me before I could even scream. And then I was lying on the floor, and I knew that I was going to die. And I knew that he was going to do things to me before I did. I was terrified."

He tried to pull away but she wouldn't let him. "Lindsay, you don't have to..."

"I know I don't. Anyway, like I said, I was really scared. And then a calm settled over me. I remembered what I believed, which was that everything *does* work out. That I'm never really alone. And I wasn't quite so scared any more."

"But Lindsay, you could have died."

She nodded. "I could have. And if I had, that would have been okay. But I didn't, and I'm very glad of that. Instead, God sent me you." She leaned forward and kissed him.

When they broke their embrace, he started to speak again but she stopped him. "Just think about what we talked about. I wouldn't have even mentioned it, but I've seen how much this all weighs on you. I just want to help."

Pulling her to him, Eric kissed her again. "I love you."

She looked at him with surprise. "You do? I mean, I love you too...God, I love you. I just..."

He smiled. "Is it that big of a shock?"

"I dunno. Maybe. Just a lot of big conversations at once. A lot to take in."

"Well, how about I take you to dinner while we absorb everything?"

She quirked an eyebrow at him. "Do you have a helicopter I don't know about?"

He grinned, shaking his head. "I noticed the kitchen in this place already has some food in it. Let's see what we can find."

Chapter Nineteen

They found a plethora of canned goods in the pantry off of the kitchen, and surprisingly, the refrigerator already had a number of items inside as well. Now that the choice was upon them, however, they had a hard time deciding on what to eat and eventually realized that they simply weren't that hungry. Deciding to come back for a larger breakfast in the morning, they only split a can of pork and beans for now, washing it down with tap water.

A quick check out the front windows showed Raziel still pacing, his limp gone, beginning to scream again before they had even reached the front vestibule. Leaving him to it, they made their way back to the day care room and their sleep mats. Curled together, Eric went to sleep quickly and found nightmares waiting for him.

There were several of them in rapid-fire succession, all of them blending together in such a fashion that upon waking it was hard to determine which parts went to which dreams. Not that it really mattered. All of them shared the same two themes. Raziel getting in and Lindsay getting hurt or killed. Both, naturally, because of something he did or failed to do.

With his sleep so troubled, waking up in the gray of early morning brought a momentary rush of relief at escaping his dreams. It was short-lived due to his realization that a man was sitting and watching them from a few feet away. Sitting up with jolt, he felt his head pulsing as he began readying himself for whatever this man would bring.

"Who are you?"

The man chuckled at him. He was bald except for a fringe of silver hair that wisped around the edge of his head and his face wore an alert but placid expression as he sat studying Eric. A pair of wire-rimmed glasses sat perched on the end of his nose, and he took them off to polish their lenses on the front of his shirt, apparently unaffected by the menace in Eric's voice. "I could ask you the same question. You are in my church after all."

"Your church?" It was then that he realized the man was wearing a priest's collar. "Oh...uh. Sorry, Father." Feeling his face flush, Eric thought about standing, but he didn't want the man to be intimidated or think he was going to attack him. "We...We weren't trying to steal anything or mess anything up. We just had some trouble with our car and needed a place to stay until morning."

The man nodded. "Much as I suspected. And I'm glad you found the door unlocked, even if it was only due to my own absent-mindedness." He stood and walked to Eric, extending his hand. "Father Hemming Park. Glad to meet you....?" He raised an inquiring eyebrow.

Shaking his hand, Eric got to his feet. "Eric. Eric Talbot. Nice to meet you. Thank you for being so understanding."

"Not at all. Glad to be of service. And to that end, if you would care to wake your friend, I've got a nice breakfast prepared for you."

"Really? That's great. I mean, thank you." He leaned down and gently shook Lindsay, who woke up right away. She blinked as she looked up at the priest, her startled expression making both Eric and Father Park laugh. "It's okay, Lindsay. He's okay with us being here. He even made us breakfast."

As they walked to the kitchen, Eric's mouth began to water as the smells of bacon and pancakes made their way to them. When they entered the room, they saw that plates full of both had already been laid out for them along with glasses of milk and a jug of maple syrup.

Father Park gestured to the chairs under the steel table at the kitchen's center. "Don't be shy. Let me know if they need to be reheated or if you need anything else."

Lindsay gave him a questioning look. "What about you? Aren't you having any?"

"Oh, I had mine while yours cooked. And I do hope you both like blueberry pancakes. They're my favorite, and I had fresh berries to put in, so I'm afraid I selfishly added them to the batter."

Eric grinned. "Sounds good to me." They both sat down and began to eat, pausing intermittently to thank the priest again for his hospitality. After they had wolfed down a few bites they began to talk about other things, and Eric tried to be casual as he asked if the priest had seen anyone else outside. The priest said he hadn't, and Eric had expected questions as to who he *should* have expected to see, but none were forthcoming. In fact, the priest asked them few questions about themselves, perhaps knowing that they would be reluctant to share and not wanting to put them in a position to lie. Instead, he talked about himself and the church, which he said would be having its first mass in less than a week.

Eric found himself liking this man and touched by his kindness. At first he had been wary of him, and he was still watchful for any surprises, wishing he could summon his ability to sense things at will and somehow determine any darkness that may lie in the priest's heart.

But that was ridiculous. If the man wanted to harm them, he could have done so while they slept. He certainly wouldn't have cooked them a delicious breakfast and made small talk.

Lindsay stifled a yawn and grinned at him from across the table. He smiled back and felt a burst of happiness at the joy she was clearly taking in their meal. There had been precious few good things he had been able to give her so far, and he was grateful for any that came, even if he couldn't really take credit.

But even in his moment of happiness he worried about Raziel. Had Father Park just been lucky or had the angel really left? It made no sense for him to give up so quickly. Likely it was a trap of some sort. Lull them into thinking he was gone so they would leave the protection of holy ground.

"Finished?"

They both nodded and the Father gave them a smile as he stood up. "Don't worry with the dishes. I'll take care of them later...I actually enjoy it. Very soothing."

Eric stood, shaking his head. "No, we'll..."

"No argument. I insist. Especially since I'm about to ask for your indulgence."

"Indulgence?"

Father Park nodded. "Yes. I have a couple of hours of phone calls that need to be made this morning before I can leave. So I would ask for your patience while I do just that. When I'm finished, I'll take you back to town. Is that alright?"

Lindsay blinked and then smiled. "Of course! But are you sure you don't mind taking us back?"

"Not at all. I'd have it no other way. In the mean time, you should feel free to go back to sleep if you like. I know it's still quite early, and I'll be poor company for the next little bit."

Eric was about to protest, but then he realized that he *was* actually still very sleepy.

Lindsay yawned again and nodded to the priest. "That actually sounds like a great idea. Thank you again for everything."

Father Park nodded and waved them off after making sure they knew how to get back to the room they had slept in before. Once there, they talked for a moment and Lindsay agreed that Raziel was probably still out there. But they also agreed that Father Park may be their best chance of escaping. They lay facing each other as they spoke, Eric's thoughts beginning to drift as he struggled to stay awake.

Lindsay was asking him if he was up to attacking Raziel again the way he had before, and he thought he said yes, but then he was gone. This time sleep was deep and black, and no dreams came.

When Eric awoke it felt as if he were climbing up from some deep, dark cave— his mind struggling to break the surface and find light again. Opening his eyes with great effort, he looked around slowly, feeling a dull worry as he noticed what looked to be afternoon sun coming through the window. The first real dread didn't set in until he realized that Lindsay wasn't there.

He slowly climbed to his feet, stumbling several times as he called out for her, the sound of his voice sounding strange in his ears. Making his way to the doorway, he looked down the hall in both directions and saw nothing. Calling out her name again, this time louder, he began working his way through the building, peering into every room he encountered.

As his fear built, so did his anger. The way he felt...it wasn't natural. The only answer was that they had been drugged. He gritted his teeth and began screaming her name, his mind reeling as he tried to make sense of it all. Could Raziel have done this? It seemed doubtful. It wasn't at all his style, and where did he suddenly come up with a henchman to fake being a priest?

So it was either "Father Park" himself or someone he worked for behind it. But why? The obvious answer was to get to him, but why not take him if that's what they were after? It made no sense.

By this point he had made his way to what appeared to be staff offices, including that of the priest, a man called Father Dorian Baxter according to the sign outside the door. All hope of finding Lindsay there gone, Eric nonetheless turned on the light and looked around the room. Then his eyes found the envelope set neatly in the center of priest's desk, his own name written in flowing letters across its front.

Ripping it open, he found a single thick sheet of paper within, a solitary line of writing upon it: *I've got her now. So come and get her. You should know the where and when. Don't come early or she dies.*

He resisted the urge to crumple or shred the paper, instead sticking it back into the envelope before putting it in his pocket. *Who* had her? And what were they talking about? He had no idea where, when, or anything else. He slammed his fist on the desk and spun around, catching himself on the door jamb before he fell. Walking more carefully, he made his way out of the office and towards the front doors of the church.

When he flung them open he squinted at the sun, now growing low in the sky. Looking down he saw Raziel back at his post, his eyes full of fire now that he saw Eric. He had no time for this. It had to end now. He was about to throw everything he had at the angel when Raziel spoke.

"They've taken her. I know all about it."

Eric took a step forward. "Where? Where the fuck did they take her? *Tell me!*"

Raziel shrugged, clearly enjoying the situation. "I don't have a clue. But I know where she *will* be, in a few days time."

"How do you know that?"

"I had a little chat with a mutual acquaintance of ours this morning. That's how I know."

Teneber. Eric gritted his teeth, wanting to launch himself at Raziel and not daring to. "Tell me then."

The angel smiled thinly, wagging a finger at him. "Now now. Not so fast. I'm not telling you anything. But I will take you there. In due time."

"Sure you will." This was getting him nowhere.

"It's true."

"Why would you do that?"

Raziel's smile widened. "Because it's where I was going to take you since the very beginning."

Eric went cold. "Teneber took her?"

Raziel looked slightly surprised. "Actually no. Someone else entirely. Somebody new, at least to me. But you'll find out all about it in due time. For now, get down here. You're going to do exactly as I say if you want to see your whore again."

Eric clenched his fists. "Maybe I should just kill you."

The angel snorted and waved his healed arm at him. "You did such a bang-up job last time. And let's say you did manage to do it. You'd never find the girl on your own. And from what I hear about the guy that's got her, after he figures out you're not coming, he'll make sure he gets his money's worth."

Lowering his head, he nodded. "Fine. Let's go then. The sooner this is all over with, the better."

"Not so fast, boy. We're not going to the party yet. Still have a few days to go. As I told you before, timing is a factor in all of this."

"What? Fuck you. We go now."

Chuckling, Raziel turned and began walking towards the corner of the church. "Still not really grasping the whole 'you have no choice but to do what I want' thing are you? We'll go when I say we go. And as for your little friend, she'll be fine til then." He snickered, shooting a look back over his shoulder at Eric. "Or at least alive."

Eric began following him. "Oh yeah? How do you know this guy won't get tired of waiting and kill her tomorrow?"

"First, because he's not going to go to all the trouble to lure you into his little trap and then kill the bait within the first 24 hours. Second, because Teneber has arranged to have him apprised of when you'll arrive. Which will be according to *our* timetable, not his."

Eric realized he didn't have any choice, at least not for the moment. As much as it maddened him, he would have to trust that Lindsay would be safe until he could get to her. "Fine. I'll do what you say."

"*Everything* I say?"

He gritted his teeth again. "Yes. Everything you say."

It sounded as if Raziel was laughing again. "Good boy."

They rounded the corner and Eric saw a large black SUV parked there. "Where'd you get the car? Is that why you were gone this morning?"

Raziel took the keys out of his pocket and unlocked the doors. "No, if you were paying attention you'd know that I was gone this morning because I had to talk with Teneber. *This* was left by the faux-priest that so easily tricked you and snatched your girl from under your nose."

Ignoring the comment, Eric climbed into the passenger side, the smell of leather and new-car smell filling his nostrils. "So how did he leave then?"

"By helicopter. Like a spy movie. It was even black."

"You watch movies?"

Raziel started the car and shrugged, his voice belying the casual gesture. "When your sole reason for existing has been taken from you, there's a lot of time to kill." He slammed the car into drive and then they were on the road.

Four hours later they were back in the Illinois countryside and pulling up outside of a farmhouse that reminded Eric of the one he had been looking at with Lindsay the day before. Swallowing hard, he gave Raziel a questioning look.

"Why're we stopping here?"

"This is going to be our little home until we have to head for the big event. Get inside." Raziel got out without waiting for a response and Eric saw no alternative but to follow suit.

They were barely on the porch before Eric heard the first sounds of buzzing. His first thought was bees, but then Raziel opened the door and the smell hit him. He gagged, backing away from the door. Raziel looked at him with amusement.

"Yeah, I know it's a little ripe, but what're you going to do? I killed the family over a week ago, but I was so busy looking for you pesky kids that I haven't had time to clean up the mess. Now get in."

"There's no way..."

"Wasn't a request. Get in now."

Holding his hand over his nose and mouth, he forced himself to enter and saw the first of the bodies lying across the living room floor. Deep gashes and tears covered the man, all of them black and writhing from the flies that worked tirelessly at the rotting flesh. Eric did vomit then, only to step in it when Raziel pushed him forward.

"Keep moving. To the kitchen."

Another body awaited them there, a young boy from the size, though too much of his face was gone to be sure. Raziel walked ahead of him to open a door next to an old-fashioned refrigerator that stood in one corner. Flipping on a light on the other side of the doorway, Raziel gestured for him to enter. As he approached, Eric saw stairs leading down into darkness.

"A basement?"

"Technically I think they used it as a fruit cellar, but you can just call it home sweet home. Now get down there."

"Why?"

The angel's eyes flashed. "Because I said so. And because I don't want to have to look at you. Go."

Shaking his head, Eric started down the stairs, shuddering at the cold of the subterranean room as he made it to the cement floor. He could just barely make out a table and a few boxes outside the circle of light given by the bulb hanging over the stairwell. Turning back to look up at the doorway, he saw Raziel's silhouette framed in the stronger light the kitchen offered.

"What now?"

Raziel reached out to the light switch and ripped it from the wall in a shower of sparks, plunging the stairs and the basement into even deeper shadow. "Lights out." With that he closed the kitchen door, making the darkness complete.

Chapter Twenty

As was often the case these days, Lindsay's first thoughts upon waking were of Eric--the anticipation of seeing him and the hope that he would feel the same. This was followed by thoughts about what they were going to do today. Out of logical sequence but no less pressing were the ponderings of where they were and what time it was.

Her eyes fluttered open onto darkness, and a quick look at her watch's glowing hands told her that it was around eight-fifteen. Then she remembered the church and felt confused, rubbing her head as she attempted to sit up and failed the first two times. Part of that was the way she felt, and the rest came from the difficulty of sitting up in the strange bed she was in. From the little she could feel and see, she decided it was probably an army cot of some kind.

Sense when? We were on the floor and...Where's Eric?

"Eric?" She called out softly, simultaneously so she wouldn't startle him from his sleep too suddenly and because she knew this was all wrong...knew that he was nowhere near. Getting no response, she swung her legs over the edge of the cot and sucked in a breath as her feet touched what felt like nylon. Even through her shoes she could feel its strange slickness and hear the zip of her sole moving along its surface.

A tent? But why?

Standing with some effort, she reached up for a roof, not finding it until she stretched on tiptoe. The same material as the floor. A tent for sure. But when had they moved to a tent?

Lindsay gasped as the zipper flap to her right was jerked down suddenly and a large bald head poked in to look at her before moving back out. She was about to move for the door when another face appeared. An older and far more frightening face.

The man would be considered distinguished-looking by many, with the long, hard features that people so often seemed to equate with intelligence and nobility. And as he edged his way through the flap, the soft purr of his chair's electric engine the only noise in this artificial womb of silent dark, she saw that he did have a certain bearing. A strong presence. She thought about King Lear, driven insane by the storm, and instead of laughing she suppressed a shiver.

If the man sensed her discomfort, he gave no indication of caring, his eyes studying her as a mean little boy's might a tortured insect. Looking for the tender spots.

He gave her a thin-lipped smile and nodded. "Hello there....Lindsay, isn't it? How're you finding your accommodations?"

She took a step back, wondering if there was another way out of the tent. "Where am I? Who are you?"

"Those things don't really matter. But suffice it to say that you are in a very old and very important place. As for myself, I'm someone who recognizes the importance of what this place represents. Someone who has an appreciation for it."

It was easy to see that this was all very wrong, and she had every idea that the man before her was totally insane. She fought the urge to take another step back and continued on.

"Where's Eric? What've you done with him?"

He laughed softly. "How clichéd can one be? Should I show you my giant laser now?" Snorting softly, he went on. "And no, that's not a sexual reference. And no, I have no laser. And no, Eric hasn't been hurt. At least not by me. Not yet."

She stepped forward again, her stomach churning. Maybe she could get around him and then get away. But there was at least one other guy out there, maybe more. A big guy. Unsure of what to do, she decided for the moment that she should just keep him talking and see what she could learn.

"Where is he then?"

The man shrugged, Lindsay realizing for the first time how large and powerful his upper body was. If he caught her as she passed by, she wouldn't even make it out to whatever guards may be waiting outside.

"I don't really know precisely. The men we had keeping you two under surveillance vanished soon after you arrived here. Disappointing, but not wholly unexpected. Not that it matters. I've already gotten word that your friend will be arriving here in just under nine days. While that is a bit long for a camping trip in my opinion, I'm unwilling to take any chances by leaving, not even for a single night. In other words, I'd make myself comfortable if I were you."

"Gotten word? What're you talking about? Does Eric know where I am?"

"I would assume so, but who can really say? All I know is that he *will* know how to get here when the time is right."

Lindsay felt her stomach tighten further at his words. *Nine days?* He couldn't know how to find her if it would really be that long. But how would he ever find out where she was? *Raziel.*

Eric would turn himself over to the angel in the hopes that he would help find her. The angel might even agree, but it would all be a lie. As late as it was, he had probably already awoken, gone outside, and bargained with Raziel. Or been killed.

She swallowed. "But...But why can't Eric come sooner? What's going on?"

The man shrugged again and waived his hand as if to dismiss the thought. "Who's to say why not sooner? He and his picked the day. Go ask them." He laughed, sounding genuinely tickled by some thought. "Just a figure of speech, of course. If you try to leave this tent, the guards have orders to shoot you. Nonlethally of course, but they're very good at their jobs. They can find all kinds of painful places, or so I've been told."

She nodded, somewhat numb due the strangeness of everything that was happening. She still had no clue how she even got here in the first place. But she had decided now that this all had far more to do with Eric than it did with her, and that only increased her worries and fears. Swallowing the foul taste in the back of her mouth, she looked at the man again.

"What do you want with Eric, anyway?"

"Eric took something of mine once. I plan on taking it back."

He smiled fully then, showing his teeth for the first time, the silver etchings spiraling around the black knives that filled his mouth seeming to give off a muted glow in the dim light the tent afforded. Then Lindsay began to scream.

Chapter Twenty-One

Lawrence rubbed his hands, willing the ache that ran through his joints like liquid fire to pass or at least dull for awhile. The arthritis had started five years ago, coming in longer and longer spurts as time had gone on. He had the best doctors, and with their treatment it had become a very occasional problem, with his hands typically enjoying the same strength and dexterity that he had grown to savor since he had begun his transformation in earnest. But there were times like now where there was nothing for it but to wait it out.

Waiting. That seemed to be all he was good for at the moment, and it galled him. Waiting for that damned boy to make his appearance. Waiting to kill that girl. Waiting to reclaim his birthright. To fulfill his destiny.

Because that was precisely what this was all about. At first he had been unsure, questioning if it were even possible to get back that which he had lost. But then he realized that he was simply being made to fight for what he wanted. It wasn't a gift, but a prize to be obtained. It was the same as alligators in a primordial swamp, fighting over a bit of meat. You bit and fought until you got what was yours. And if you didn't...well, you didn't have anybody to blame but yourself, did you?

But he was a winner. He always had been. Despite his childhood, full of cold stares and solitude, he had grown strong. Heedless of an accident that would have ended most people, he had compensated for his loss and grown fearless. Dangerous. Powerful. Ready for the kiss of his god.

There was only one more obstacle between him and what was his, and that was the boy. A simple-minded and worthless boy that had the misfortune of being a footnote in Lawrence's life. The thought that all these years and his entire future rested on his meeting with this child made him want to laugh and scream. It was maddening, insulting, and utterly hilarious.

But he had to take the boy seriously, at least for the moment. He had learned enough to know that he had some power at least, and while he doubted he had much skill at using it, he would still be extremely dangerous under the wrong circumstances.

Running his tongue gingerly over his black teeth, he rolled down the path that led to the cave entrance, the night sky laid out before him like a blanket of dreams, full of twinkling wishes and hopes that filled his heart with a dark yearning memory. Soon it would all be gone. Smiling as a delicious shiver passed through him, he passed through the mouth of the cave, the cold desert air warming slightly as he passed by the first of numerous lighting arrays that lined the walls going down into the earth.

He felt his mood begin to lighten as he went deeper, his impatience giving way to acceptance that it was all necessary. His first thought when he got the report that the boy and his whore were at the church had been to take them both while they lay drugged. But then he realized that he couldn't risk the boy waking up before they reached the site. He would likely kill all of the guards and the element of surprise would be gone.

No, better to get the bait and set the trap. And then wait. He snorted as he thought again of the indignity he was forced to suffer, having to wrest away this power from a child. The very fact that his banal piece of ass could serve as bait in the first place was only further evidence of how unsuitable the boy was to be the bearer of his god's blessing.

But it was all of no consequence. It was all just part of his rite of passage. He knew that for certain now. Because of the dreams.

They had started his first night here—the same night that he had learned that the boy and girl were hiding in the church from some man who appeared to be trying to kill them and was certainly more than human. He had found this news to be extremely troubling, and he had thought at first he would never find sleep again.

To his surprise, he had drifted off easily, only to awaken in a great ballroom, the midnight sky painted on the ceiling, swirling out from the large moon that lay at the center of everything. The man in the moon tipped him a knowing wink while smiling an unpleasant smile that made Lawrence nervous in spite of himself. He was lying on a highly-polished hardwood floor, and it wasn't until he stood up that he knew he must be dreaming.

"Nice, isn't it?"

Lawrence had spun around to see a man walking towards him, his neatly-pressed suit a pure and dazzling white and his face slightly out-of-focus. Then he realized that *everything* about the man was out of focus. He would sometimes think there was no one there, but then he would remember that he was talking to somebody after all.

"What's nice?"

He thought the man smiled. "Standing on your own two feet. Been awhile for you."

He nodded, his eyes narrowing. "Yes. Who are you?"

"I'm a friend, Lawrence. And a guide. A helping hand to help you get what you want."

"What I want? What do you know about what I want?" Even as he asked the questions and felt the anger behind them, he felt foolish, remembering again for a moment that this was only a dream. But still...

"Why, you want the power of the Darkness don't you?"

The Darkness. That was his god's name then. He wanted to cry for joy, but he swallowed his tears and clearing his throat, tried to maintain control.

"What do you know about it?"

"Why, I am its servant. And I'm here to give you some advice."

"Advice?"

The man chuckled. "This will go quicker if you don't repeat everything I say. But yes. The advice is this: Wait here for the boy. Let him come in his own time. If you do this, you will find him coming to you in a little over a week."

Lawrence felt a thrill of excitement, unsure of whether or not he could believe any of this. It could all just be the product of wishful thinking. But it all felt so *real*.

"So what do I do in the mean time?"

He had woken then, jolted awake by some noise outside his tent. He didn't go back to sleep this time, his stomach fluttering with excitement as he went back over the dream again and again in his mind and waited for morning.

In the days that followed, the dreams had continued to come. The new dreams had seemed no less real, but they were a great deal more confusing than that of the first night. Most involved flashes of violence or betrayal, though a few seemed peaceful as far as he could see. In one, a handsome middle-aged man sat in an office talking to a teenaged boy. In another, what looked to be a truck driver sat in his rig on the side of some highway, a distant look in his eyes as he looked into the fading light.

There seemed to be no rhyme or reason to what he was shown, all of it a jumble of images or experiences, moments plucked out of time from lives that he had never lived. Every dream was something different, though the presentation never really varied. A whirlwind of misfortunes, a storm of hatred. And him in the center of it all, laughing like a child.

He had reached the main chamber now, the full bed he had set up atop the stone shelf in the room's center turned down and waiting. Leaning forward as he drove up the ramp that had been put in the day they had arrived, he could feel his heart racing. Easing himself from the chair into the bed, he looked around in the semi-darkness of the chamber, his breath catching for a moment at the overwhelming grandness of it all. He was doing it. He was going to make it happen.

He smiled to himself as he began to slip into sleep, his thundering heart and his speeding thoughts slowing down as his consciousness began to dissolve. Soon he was deep asleep and dreaming his dreams again, mindless of the shadows that rose and fell around the edge of the room. He slumbered on, comforted by the cool, musty silence of the church in which he lay. His dreams were black and deep.

Chapter Twenty-Two

There is a kind of sleep that comes with sickness of the body, a consequence of the natural infirmities that are inherent in a prolonged illness or extended period of being inactive. Then there is the kind of sleep that comes with sickness of the soul. Sleep born out of despair.

The conditions in the basement had left much to be desired from the standpoint of physical comforts to be sure. The air was stale and almost painfully cool, the faint smell of waste from the bucket he had been left as a toilet wafting over whenever he made the mistake of venturing too near. The days were swathed in shadow, with the only light or fresh air coming from two tiny windows near the ceiling that he had propped open. They had been painted black to block out all light back when the room had been a proper fruit cellar, and he had been well into his second day before he even noticed them. Now they were his only tether to the outside world, his only way of marking the passage of days. There had been eight of them so far.

There was no bed or chair to be had, but he had found a few old and spidery blankets that he had spread down on the concrete floor as a makeshift bed. The cold cut through them to spread through his body like a disease, settling into his joints and making him shiver in the dark.

He got food twice a day—canned beans or soup, usually, and neither actually cooked. Raziel had made little mocking comments at first, but even that had faded with time. He didn't know if the charm had gone out of it or if the angel just didn't think he was worth the effort any more.

There was nothing to do but sleep and think, and as the days went on everything began to blur and bleed into each other as sleep became more and more of a constant. While he was somewhat sick and weak, that wasn't his true concern. The deep black that lulled him to sleep came from within, growing steadily as his hope's flame flickered and guttered more with every passing hour.

His hopelessness had come on slowly, stealthily stealing across his heart like the shadows that crawled across the cinder block walls of this place as day faded into night. He had felt several moments of rebellion and anger, thinking that Raziel would never take him to Lindsay or that he should force Raziel to take him now. But he knew that Raziel was telling the truth, or at least part of the truth. And he had every belief that no amount of intimidation or torture would make Raziel tell him where Lindsay was. Eric suspected that the angel's hatred for him far outstripped any desire for self-preservation. That was if he could overtake him in the first place, which was far from a certain thing.

So he slept. And ate occasionally. And tried to think of a better plan than waiting. And failed. And tried to think of what he should do in the various scenarios he imagined might play out when he finally got out of this room and back near Lindsay. And tried to see one that ended well.

Eight days in, he sat against a bare, unpainted wall, staring up at the light filtering in through the propped open window slits in the opposite wall. He itched constantly, his hair greasy and his face dirty and raw. A rib-bruising cough slammed his back into the wall and he wondered not for the first time if he had pneumonia. Looking up at the window again, he took in a deep breath and smelled honeysuckle in the air. The sweet smell bloomed in his brain, and before he knew it he was crying.

He was just so tired of everything. Tired of trying so hard to do the right thing and be a good person and failing so miserably at it. Tired of hurting people, particularly those he cared about. It was his fault his father was dead, and it was his fault that Lindsay was going through whatever was happening to her. And what good was he to her? To anyone? To himself? Even with whatever power he seemed to have, he hadn't actually helped anything. He hadn't done anything but be a victim.

A deep and abiding loneliness swept through him then, a dark shape passing just under the surface and causing him to weep again. He had lost everything and he didn't understand why. None of it made any sense at all.

He began thinking of what Lindsay had said before she was taken, when she was talking about God and what she believed. That everything happened for a reason and that we should be grateful for everything. That there was a purpose for every single thing. Even him.

Thinking of her made his chest feel as though it would cave in from some unseen weight, but it also made him think of something he hadn't before. That perhaps it wasn't all his fault. Perhaps he was doing the best he could with the cards he had been dealt, and that those cards *had* been dealt for a reason. And perhaps he really wasn't alone.

This thought was both alien and familiar, his breath catching in his throat as he closed his eyes and tried to pin down what he was feeling. Searching himself, he found a voice that was not his own, telling him that everything could still turn out all right. And that he was never alone. He felt a thrill run through him, terrifying and joyous, as he realized that this voice and the presence behind it was telling the truth and that it had *always* been there, waiting to be heard. He had spent his life worrying and blaming himself for every bad thing that happened in his life, always unwilling to turn to anyone else to help with the obstacles he faced. Never realizing that there was an alternative to doing everything alone.

Then Eric did something that he hadn't done in a very long time. He moved to kneel upon his knees, lines of sunlight touching his face as he lowered his head and closed his eyes. Then he began to pray.

"Please Lord. I don't know what to tell you. But I'm in bad trouble. Lindsay is too. I don't know what to do and I don't know how to help things. They tell me that when I die it's going to end everything. I...I don't understand how that can be true. Why you would allow that to happen. But I know that I have to just trust you. That things will work out.

"It's hard though, you know? I worry, and I try, and...things just don't work out. I just make things worse. Even after all of this, I really don't even know what's going on, or why I'm the one picked for this.

"I know this just sounds like I'm bitc...complaining and whining and stuff, but I'm not....Well, I am...but I'm grateful for my life and for all the things in it. I am. But I need help. I need help in understanding and I need help in doing the right thing. Please Lord, please help me. Help me."

Eric moved back to a sitting position, leaning against the wall as he went over the words in his head. He felt somewhat better now, but it would take more than an improved mood to save himself and Lindsay. He thought about praying again, trying to do a better job, but ultimately decided that it was a stupid idea. He had said what he had needed to say, and it was ridiculous to think that better phrasing would help things further.

Laughing to himself, he eased back down onto the blankets, a calm settling over him as he drifted back to sleep. He was still cold and miserable, but he thought he felt a little more hopeful. And a little less alone.

Eric woke up with a start, his eyes wide as he sat up straight. He had been dreaming something. *Something.* What was it? It was important whatever it was. It had seemed like a flash of memory, but no memory that he had ever known.

He rubbed his face and looked around, the dim light coming through the windows turning gray as a thick patch of clouds passed in front of the sun. *What had it been?* Whatever it had been, it seemed to be gone now. Shaking his head, he began to stand when he froze mid-motion, easing himself back down to the ground like a man in a trance. He remembered something. A tiny keystone had been removed from a dam of memory inside him, and he felt a steady trickle of remembrance filling his mind, building faster as more stones lost their grip. He stared into space blankly, his attention raptly held by the dam's breaking and the flood of memory that accompanied it. Eric began seizing then, his body thrashing as his back arched to the edge of breaking and his muscles corded into knots thick and hard. Like a silent dance, he jerked and twisted for nearly ten minutes as the flood waters were absorbed and that which they bore was reconciled. Slowly he began to still, his awareness of the room around him once again becoming more than a hazy dream.

Moving gingerly, he sat up as a realization blazed across his brain. He was starting to remember everything. Everything.

He smiled.

Chapter Twenty-Three

Raziel stood up in the knee-high grass that covered the lawn of the old farmhouse, looking at the building with mild distaste. As much as he could relish violence while in the heat of his anger, he hated witnessing the aftermath and smelling the cloying scent of death that hung heavy in the air of the place. Besides, he could guard the boy just as easily from out here as from inside.

He felt his mood improving now that the final stretch of this journey was upon them. When first told that he would have to wait even longer to dispense with the boy he had been in a rage. He was tired of waiting, and Teneber had never given him a clear explanation of why time was such a factor, saying only that it was a crucial element of the process.

But in the end his fear of Teneber had stilled his tongue and he had agreed to wait and come when called. Like the good little dog that he was.

Raziel wanted to pound the earth at the thought but knew how futile and pathetic the gesture would be. He *was* a dog now--afraid of base, unholy creatures and doing their bidding. Brought low into quivering servitude in a feeble attempt to secure his revenge and survival. All because his Master, his Lord, had saw fit to abandon him.

This thought brought bile worse than any other, filling him with a wretched loathing and anger that only grew worse over time. He had served the Lord perfectly, and yet he was punished. Somehow the High had seen fit to allow an *abomination* like the creature he had killed at the institution to exist. Had let its foul power slaughter countless innocents. And yet He saw fit to judge His own true and loyal servant when he simply destroyed what had been a blight upon his Master's creation.

To him this was a great paradox, and the illogic of it all had tormented him for years. But then, when he had least expected it, the answer had finally come to him. It had been in the damned town of Deritus, as he was forced again to see a pit of writhing evil that the High had not seen fit to wipe out or even curb. Tired and bleeding, missing flesh in a hundred places, he had ripped the head from the last clawing body, having learned from the past few weeks' experience that it was the only way to guarantee these monsters would not return.

It was then, as the last corpse tumbled to the ground, that he had looked up into the night sky--clear and full of stars so beautiful that it would have taken his breath if he had it to give. Standing in the midst of that abattoir, broken and bleeding, he found an end to the conflict that had tormented him so.

There *was* no excuse for the evil God allowed. There was no purpose to anything beyond perhaps some sadistic clockwork that God Himself had set in motion millennia before. There was no justification for his own expulsion from Heaven. God was a hypocrite.

And with this thought came a kind of peace. The knowledge that while the path behind him was barred, the one before him was clear.

Now, walking to the house, Raziel firmed his resolve to complete this thing. He would forge his purpose with his own will and make the best of what he had. If he survived the death of the boy, a new world would lie before him, and perhaps in that world he would find a place where he truly belonged.

Opening the door to the basement, he felt mild surprise run through him as he saw Eric looking up at him from the foot of the steps, his eyes narrow against the light.

"Get up here. It's time to go."

Eric nodded without another word and began to climb, his face calm as he rose. Raziel gave him a shove that made the boy stumble as he passed, but Eric said nothing. Five minutes later they were in the SUV and headed along the road to their final destination.

They had been on the road for only a few minutes when Raziel realized that he was worried. He had been casting glances at the boy since they had started driving, unable to let go of the idea that something was different. Eric seemed calmer and more sure of himself now. It wasn't in anything he said--the boy hadn't spoken at all, in fact—but instead it was more in the way he carried himself. The way he would look at Raziel occasionally, as if weighing him. Judging him. Perhaps he had concocted some grand plan down in his little prison, and he was busy gloating over how clever he was. The little fool.

He did not think that God would come to the boy's rescue either. He had seen and gone through too much to believe otherwise. And it was on Him, not Raziel, that all had come to pass as it had. And when he killed the boy and brought forth the end of everything, that blood would be on His hands as well.

Chapter Twenty-Four

Eric watched the mile markers rolling by, willing the time to pass more quickly until he could see Lindsay again. He knew now that it was no trick of Raziel's that had brought him out of the basement, and he knew that the angel was taking him directly to where the madman held her. What he found so frustrating was that he still didn't know where the place was—just one of many blank spots that remained in his mind. The worst part was for a moment, as the dam had broken, he *had* known. But his mind was still adjusting it seemed, reorganizing and making room in the wake of all that had happened in the past few hours. So for now, despite everything, he was still forced to rely on Raziel to get him to Lindsay.

Looking over at the angel, Eric felt the usual anger rise, but also a measure of pity. It was that same pity that led him to speak after a moment of considering silence.

"Raziel, why are you doing this?"

Several seconds passed by, and Eric was beginning to think that he wasn't going to receive any response at all. Then it came, Raziel's voice hoarse and bitter.

"You know why. For revenge. Because that is all that's been left to me."

Eric frowned and looked out the window again. "That's not true. Have you ever tried to ask for forgiveness?"

The angel snorted. "Forgiveness? I'm sick of the word. What did I do that needed to be forgiven? Destroy evil? Clean up God's messes for Him? Serve Him blindly and loyally just so He could kick me like a dog?"

He turned back to Raziel, his eyes dark but kind. "You disobeyed God. You went against His Will. That doesn't sound wrong to you?"

The angel shot him a fiery look as he sped past a slow moving car on the highway. "What do *you* know about God's Will? Or about serving him? All you are is a self-absorbed little meat bomb that is toting Armageddon around in its belly. I don't need a lecture from you. From anyone."

Eric's expression didn't change. "I'm not saying you're wrong about me. But I'm not lecturing you. Just trying to understand. You know that God exists. You've served Him and been in His presence. Why would you throw it all away? Why wouldn't you try to get it back?"

The leather on the steering wheel groaned and split as Raziel gripped it hard. "I didn't throw anything away." He said through clenched teeth. "I was *thrown* away. For doing what I thought was best when a choice was upon me. And I won't crawl back to Him after that."

"No, you did what you *wanted* to do. You knew what your duty was, what His Will was, and you went against it. But you know, I don't really think that was the problem..."

"Shut up! I don't want to hear another word out of you."

"...No, the problem was when you were so proud and so cowardly that you made a deal with evil against God. Instead of asking for forgiveness, you rebelled. Instead of feeling remorse, you chose self-righteous anger and hatred instead. God never abandoned you..."

"Shut up! Shut up! Shut up!"

"....You abandoned Him."

Raziel slammed the brakes, sending the car into a skid that left them in a cloud of dust when the car finally screeched to a halt.

"If you don't shut up, I'll gag you for the rest of the trip. I won't listen to your sanctimonious preaching any longer. I choose my life, and I won't be judged by you or anyone. Not even Him. Not anymore."

Eric looked at him intently, knowing the words were earnest. He felt a sadness bloom in his heart like a dark flower—sadness for Raziel and all that had been lost. But the angel had made his choice. Nodding, he turned to the window again.

"I believe you. I won't ask about it again."

Raziel started forward again without another word, driving even faster now as dusk approached. It seemed the angel was as anxious to reach their destination as he was.

Closing his eyes, he sank quickly into a light and troubled sleep.

Even with Raziel's constant speeding, it was nearly fourteen hours before they reached the access road and gatehouse that led to their destination. They had been in Texas for over two hours at that point, far from anything even approaching a town. The last gas station had been nearly an hour ago, the third of their five-minute stops along the way to refuel.

A pair of armed guards had awaited them at the gatehouse which lay five minutes down the dusty desert road, their faces hard and deadly as they had peered into the car. They had both glanced at Raziel, but it was clear that their real focus was on Eric, and after a moment they opened the gate and let them pass.

They had driven for another ten minutes before Raziel stopped the car, getting out without another word. Eric peered outside his dirty window and noticed a path cutting away from the road, marked by an orange stake on either side. Getting out, he barely felt the cold morning air as he looked at Raziel.

"So what now?"

The angel smirked and pointed to the path. "We head this way until we reach the spot where I get to end you and you get to murder the world. That's what now."

Eric nodded. "That's what I thought. This close, I can feel the place a little."

"Good for you. Get moving."

He looked at Raziel, his face solemn. "Raziel, I'm sorry that things happened the way they did with you. That you became what you did. But I can't waste any more time with you."

Raziel's face twisted into a mask of fury. "What are..." His words became a scream of agony as darkness sprang up and consumed him, destroying and devouring every last part of him utterly with a terrifying swiftness. It was over in a handful of moments, his footprints the only sign that he had ever been there at all.

Without looking back, Eric began running up the path ahead of him.

Part III: Darkness

Chapter Twenty-Five

Damsel in distress. A fucking damsel in fucking distress. Even after everything she had been through and overcome, Lindsay still found herself filling the same role. And whatever it might say about her, whatever blow it might be to her pride, none of that mattered. What *did* matter was that she was bait. Bait to lure Eric into a trap.

She sat with her back against a wall of the large chamber that, judging from the massive bed that had been moved over to a corner several hours ago, the monster had been using for a bedroom before today. Her hands were bound behind her with thick nylon cord and her feet were tied with the same. Back and shoulders aching from sitting in the same awkward and uncomfortable position for hours, she tried to flex and shift her muscles to keep them loose. It may be that she would be unable to do anything when the time came, but that didn't mean she wouldn't try.

In the days since her first encounter with the man that had abducted her, she had only seen him once more before today. That had been three days ago, when he had rolled into her tent silently, staring at her for several minutes, his eyes roving over her hungrily, before disappearing through the flap again without uttering a word. She had waited for over an hour after he had left, certain that at any moment he would scuttle back into the tent and attack her. She could see in his eyes that he wanted to do so badly. But he had never come.

Whatever held him in check, be it fear or belief, had apparently been made to apply to his help as well. There was more than one time that she heard a guard pass by her tent murmuring what he would do to her, and delivery of her meals were often accompanied by various uncreative gestures and invitations. She stayed tensed and ready to defend herself for when the time finally came, but it never did.

And now today. Yanked roughly from her cot just before sunrise, fed another day's worth of cold eggs and sausage, and then bound and made to sit here in this cave. She sat only fifteen feet or so from the entrance to the chamber, and she craned her neck at every little sound, hoping for a glimpse of Eric, wanting to warn him. Warn him of what, she wasn't certain.

Eric would know it was a trap before he came, of course. And he wouldn't care. He would do whatever it took to get her back, and he wouldn't see the danger until it was too late.

Lindsay saw where the real danger lay. The past few days had told her that her abductor had at least twenty armed men with him, but that only concerned her a little. It was the little old man, perched upon the enormous stone at the room's center that frightened her the most. Face tight with expectation like a child on

Christmas morning, she knew if anything proved to be Eric's undoing, it would be him. It sounded ridiculous, but she knew it was so.

So she would do whatever she could to help Eric get away, to keep him safe. She was still trying to settle on what she should yell to him when she saw him when the crackle of a walkie-talkie made her jump. She looked up to see the monster listening to someone on the other end, a terrible black smile spreading across his face.

"Excellent, excellent. Remember, let him through without any trouble, and *no one* but him is to come into the cave without my word. Understood?"

The thought of the old man being alone against the two of them should have comforted Lindsay, but somehow it didn't. He was insane to be sure, but he seemed so *certain* of things as well. So sure that he would win.

Still, perhaps if Raziel came along it could work to their advantage. Maybe. She started again as she realized that the monster was staring at her intently from the edge of the stone.

"Your love will be here soon, girl. Get ready to say your goodbyes."

Chapter Twenty-Six

Eric leaned over, his hands on his knees, gasping as he struggled to stay on his feet. He hadn't realized how sick he had grown during his time in the basement, but he knew it now. Breath coming in shuddering wheezes, he fought the blackness that threatened to swallow his vision as he steadied himself and started forward again, this time more slowly.

The path had not been an extremely hard one, and at first he had run and then jogged along without much problem. But within five minutes the exertion had taken its toll and he had fallen for the first of several times, scraping his arms as he tried to catch himself. Since the last fall he had settled for a fast walk, and even that had proved taxing. So it was with more than a little relief that he climbed the last peak and saw the cave entrance, four men armed with assault rifles standing nearby.

They saw him immediately, appearing unsurprised as they swung towards him. One of them, a giant of a man with a blond buzzcut, moved to speak, but he never had the chance. The next moment all four of them had exploded in a ebony mist of blood and bone. Eric reached out, and feeling no others nearby, moved on to the entrance of the cave.

The way was well-lit by electric lights strung along the walls of tunnel, the glowing line traveling deeper into the earth as they went. He followed them slowly, his hand moving along the rocky wall for balance, his breath still coming in gasps. Aside from his physical weakness, he was somewhat disoriented being in this place, impressions from its dark past reverberating through him as he moved farther underground. Forcing it all away, he gritted his teeth and slowed his breath, focusing on the next light and then the next. And then the next. And then the last.

When the trail of lights ended, he wondered for a moment if he had taken a wrong turn somehow, though he didn't believe that to be the case. Reaching out, he could sense someone a short distance ahead of him. Lindsay.

He started moving forward again, leaving the wall behind, and as he turned a corner he saw firelight dancing along the tunnel. He considered pausing, but he doubted that surprise was an option. Getting to Lindsay was what was important now.

Walking out into the large chamber, he was momentarily assailed again with flashes of ancient times filled with fear and dark ritual. He stumbled before pushing them away and regaining his balance. Turning as soon as he recovered, he saw Lindsay and began to move towards her when she screamed to him.

"Eric, no! He's going to kill you! Get away! Just....just get away!" The plaintive sound of her voice, the fear and hopelessness he heard there, made him draw up short. He saw that she was looking past him, and he turned to find the object of her fear.

The crippled man was smiling at him wickedly, his black razor teeth seeming to move and shift in the shadows from the fire. As the only source of light came from a large brazier that sat atop the stone platform the man was on, he could not make out his features entirely, but what he could see conveyed gleeful arrogance. But none of that would have troubled Eric if not for something else. Despite having reached out to sense the chamber before entering, he hadn't known the man was there in the first place.

Lawrence gripped the arms of his chair tightly, fighting the urge to spring from it and tear the stupid expression from the half-wit's face where he stood. *This* was the usurper of his destiny? *This* was the obstacle in his path? The one that had been chosen to replace *him*? Even after seeing pictures and video, reading backgrounds and reports, none of it had prepared him for the insult of reality. He had been passed over for a boy. A stupid, average *boy*.

But still. He had to be careful here, and make every move with deliberate care. He had no clear idea just how dangerous the boy would be, and while he knew he would be victorious, he wanted to ensure that when he tore the life from this child that it was done with minimal complications.

Smiling again, he pulled up to the edge of the stone and looked at the boy, their eyes at equal height in this position.

"Greetings, Eric. How nice of you to join us." He gestured to the ramp that led up to the stone's surface. "Why don't you come up here and meet me properly."

Eric shot him a dark look of anger and incredulity. "Why don't you get fucked. Count yourself lucky if I don't kill you. For now I'm taking Lindsay and leaving."

He felt himself bristling and forced his anger into check. "My boy, I wasn't really asking. One call from me and there will be twenty machine guns in here pointed at your head."

"Sixteen."

Lawrence blinked. "What?"

Eric moved to Lindsay and began trying to undo the knots binding her hands. "It'd be sixteen. I killed the four outside of here. And I'll do the same with the others... and you... if you try anything."

Lawrence struggled to hide his surprise. "I see. How interesting. But perhaps *this* will interest *you*. Your little whore there has had breakfast every morning regular as clockwork for the past week. She always cleans her plate like a good girl, and this morning was no different. Except for the fact that her food contained enough nerve toxin to kill her ten times over."

Eric stopped and looked up at him, his face hard. "You're lying." The girl was looking between them, the color gone from her face.

He shook his head. "I'm afraid not, my boy. It's time-released, and she has around, oh, eight or nine more hours before it'll actually kick in. But if she doesn't have the counteragent in her bloodstream by then, she'll be frothing and clawing at her eyes for several minutes before she actually dies." He paused, letting the words sink in. "I don't lie, and I don't bluff. Do you actually think I would go to all this trouble to risk you just walking away?"

Eric stood, his fists clenched at his sides. "Give it to her or I'll tear you apart slowly. You should know that I can."

"Threatening me is quite pointless. I will get what I want in this, of that you can be assured. I am willing to risk everything, including my life. You, on the other hand, are unwilling to risk hers. So do as I say and quit wasting my time."

Eric's lips drew back from his teeth in a snarl and Lawrence felt a thrill of fear, knowing suddenly that he had misjudged the situation. He had gone too far, and now he was going to die.

He reached out, intending to shatter the man's left hand, and to keep breaking and rending parts of him until he gave Eric the antidote he needed. But nothing happened. It wasn't as if he had lost the power—he could still feel it within him and could feel it stretching out towards the man. But it was as if it could find nothing but thin air when it reached him. He tried again, but it was the same.

His mind racing, Eric walked to the ramp and moved up onto the stone platform as he tried to make sense of what was happening. The man had moved his chair closer to the center of the stone as he had ascended, and now he could see him more clearly. He was an older man, prematurely aged further by his condition and the cruelty that lay in his heart. Eric could see silver etching on his black teeth in this light, and the glowing characters seemed strangely familiar to him. Not that it mattered. He just had to look for a way to gain the advantage.

"My name is Lawrence Hobbes, Eric. I've been watching you for a fairly short time, but I suppose you could say that I've been looking for you all of your life and more."

"Is that so?"

Lawrence nodded. "It is. You, or at least what you represent. A way to reclaim what should have been mine. What *is* mine."

Eric drew closer slowly. If he could move quick enough, he could grab the man and hopefully force him to give them the antidote. He didn't care what he had to do to him.

"That's close enough, boy. No tricks now. Not when we're just now getting acquainted." He gave Eric a hard look before gesturing to the cavern. "Do you know what this is?"

Eric glanced around, the words coming to his lips before he thought. "It's an evil place. It was a kind of church once. A ritual place."

The man gave that ghastly smile again and chuckled. "Yes, quite so. It was used by a very obscure cult that had been banished from the Pawnee tribes far north of here. They worshipped a dark god they called Evening Star. Apparently they got very muddled and murky with their beliefs, making up some bizarre apocalyptic mythos that has no basis in reality whatsoever. But still, their hearts were in the right place." He laughed. "And the core beliefs were sound enough, even if we call Evening Star by another name."

Eric felt anger and shame well up in him. "The Darkness."

"Yes. The Darkness. And this was their most revered church and temple. A suitable place for a sacrifice. A good spot to prove one's faith."

He took another step forward. "Why are you doing this? What do you want from me?"

Lawrence flicked a switch on the side of the gas-powered brazier, plunging the chamber into darkness.

"I want you to scream for me before you die."

Chapter Twenty-Seven

Eric had loosened the ropes tying Lindsay's arms only slightly, but she was trying to take advantage of it nonetheless, frantically working her hands and wrists to no avail. While she had worked, her hands had bumped into a small horn of rock that jutted out from the wall behind her, and now she tried to use that to further loosen the knots.

Her heart slammed in her chest as she squinted in the darkness, unable to see anything. She wanted to call out to Eric, but she couldn't risk distracting him. He had remained silent for his part, and the only sound she had heard aside from her own desperate movements was the creak of the wheelchair followed by the stealthy sound of Lawrence Hobbes moving to the ground.

Even using the rock, she was making little to no progress. She began tugging harder, and it was during one of the tugs that her hand hit the sandy ground at the base of the wall and she felt her fingers brush something cold and hard down in the earth. Without pausing to think or question, she began digging deeper.

Eric walked slowly and quietly, moving in a circle so as to not fall off the edge of the platform. His first thought had been to get to Lindsay, but he knew she would yell if Hobbes went for her, and he didn't want to lead the maniac to her. Besides, he had every idea that he was the only thing the other man had in mind.

He reached out again, trying to sense the other man and finding nothing. It was more than a little ironic that he couldn't even see in the dark given all that had transpired. If he got killed because of this it would be more than a little frustrating.

He heard a quiet rustle that sounded like something soft sliding over stone and he remembered the strange leather harness he had seen Hobbes wearing. It had seemed to come from his left, but he couldn't be certain. The key was to be...

The air went out of him when he hit the ground, his legs jerked out from under him neatly. Somehow the man had gotten behind him, and even as he rolled onto his back he felt the other's weight bearing down on his legs and then stomach, pushing the air out of him again.

Hobbes was puffing like an excited animal now, his teeth clicking repeatedly as he worked his way up Eric's body. He tried to fight him off, but the man pinned his arms easily using his body and one hand while the other found its way to his throat.

Even as he felt his windpipe begin to give, he tried to roll and throw Hobbes from him, but it was no use. The past few days had left him too weak, and Hobbes was too strong. He flung his head about in a vain attempt to struggle even as he felt himself starting to black out.

Then a searing pain stabbed into his shoulder as Hobbes bit down, tearing a chunk of meat away as he yanked his head back, gulping it down. After swallowing, he began to whisper feverishly to Eric in the dark.

"It's mine, it's mine, it's mine, it's mine..." He began to squeeze his throat tighter.

Forcing his last bit of air out, he called out as loud as he could. "Lindsay, get away..."

He was surprised when he heard her voice close by. "Not hardly. Take this." He heard something clatter near his left hand and he clawed desperately for it even as Hobbes tightened his grip on his wrist. Everything was growing cottony, and he knew he wouldn't find whatever it was in time.

Then his fingers touched on something hard. He thrust his hand forward enough to grasp it, knowing it was a knife as soon as he gripped it. Twisting his hand he managed to stab it into Hobbes' forearm, doubting it would be enough.

To his surprise, the man let out a howl of pain and shock, his iron grip disappearing momentarily from his wrist and his throat as he gripped his wound. Eric didn't wait. He thrust the knife just below where he had heard the scream and felt it push into something wet and yielding. Grimacing, he shoved it further in as Hobbes began to make a gurgling sound.

This time he managed to roll Hobbes from atop him, and with both arms free he got to his knees, choking and wheezing as he searched for Hobbes and found him. Finding the hilt of the knife where it was buried in the man's throat, he twisted it sideways before yanking it free, only to bring it down again with both hands into the man's face and plunging it deep. Giving a final shudder, Lawrence Hobbes grew still.

Yanking the knife free again, Eric moved to where he had last heard Lindsay's voice. "You okay?" His voice came out a hoarse whisper, but it seemed to boom in the black.

He heard her gasp and start crying. "Yes...oh God...are *you* okay? Is he still alive?"

Eric shook his head and then realized she couldn't see it. "No. He's dead. And yeah. I'm okay. We'll be okay now."

She was silent for a moment and he knew what she was thinking before she spoke. "What about what he said before? About the poison?"

He eased over the side of the stone, dropping to the chamber floor next to her. Setting the knife down, he found her face in the dark and caressed it, kissing her softly.

"Don't worry. Hobbes didn't do that to you. He was never science-minded. He had one of his men do it, if he's not lying about the whole thing. And I'll make them give you the antidote."

She trembled slightly against his hand. "How?"
"By torturing and killing them until they do."

Chapter Twenty-Eight

There is a trust that must exist between two people, even the barest of acquaintances. When the relationship is much more, when two people are so truly and deeply connected that the other person is a natural inclusion in every thought, that trust must be infinitely stronger and more durable to support the weight of all that might be thrust upon it. It must be the finest, most flexible steel—able to weather the worst of suspicions and the most terrible of doubts. Unbreakable.

It was that trust that Eric hoped existed between himself and Lindsay, and it was that strength and patience that he asked for from her in the weeks and months that followed. If fear that he was asking too much was his constant companion (and it was), it was his fault and not hers.

The day in the cave had stayed with him for a long time, and in truth would always be with him. Lindsay told him later that Hobbes' boasts of twenty or more men had been legitimate, but he had only found three left despite all his hunting. He had taken Lindsay with him for fear of the men discovering her if left behind, and she was there to bear witness to the things he did to those men in an effort to learn of an antidote. To her credit, she watched it all without growing sick, and to his, he didn't kill anyone else.

But in the end, all he got were blank stares and tearful professions of ignorance. There were no medical or scientific staff with them. There never had been. There weren't even any medical supplies aside from some personal medication of Hobbes' and a well-stocked first aid kit for the men. No antidote.

Perhaps no poison either. But Eric was unwilling to risk that without exhausting every last avenue. After the last man had been sent out into the desert, they went to Hobbes tent and went through everything, finding his bag of pills and seeing nothing beyond pain medication and heart medicine. Then they searched the other tents and supplies and found nothing.

By three they had gone through everything twice and Eric was trembling on the edge of collapse, his body racked by coughs and wheezes as he shuffled along. Lindsay called an end to it then, convincing him that they had done all they could, and all that was left was to wait it out and see.

He reluctantly agreed, and taking a truck out to Raziel's vehicle, they headed east towards Dallas. When they arrived on the outskirts of the city three hours later, Lindsay said she still felt fine. Despite his protests she had driven the entire way, insisting that he needed rest and that she would be fine.

That night had been the longest of his life. During their search of the camp they had found a lockbox containing a little over a hundred thousand in cash secreted away in Hobbes' tent, and they had gotten a nice hotel room and ordered room service. The food sat cold and uneaten, the two of them holding each other as they lay on the bed talking as the minutes ticked by. They talked some about what had happened, but it was still too fresh to dwell on for very long. So they talked about other things, telling funny stories and making plans for what they would do now that they were free of Raziel and Lawrence Hobbes. And though Eric could hear what was left unspoken clearly, he knew well enough to leave it alone for the moment.

And so the night went, and at some point she fell asleep and he watched over her, guarding her breath and treasuring her face. Dawn was just spilling over their bed when he brushed the hair from her face, causing her to stir. Smiling, he leaned down to whisper to her.

"You're still here."

She opened her eyes and smiled at him, and the joy and relief he saw in her face blurred his vision for a moment. Wiping his eyes, she laughed.

"You're such a pessimist. I knew that old fart was lying the whole time."

"You were probably in on it with him. You do have a history of faking fatal conditions."

Lindsay gasped, feigning shock. "Once! I faked cancer once and you'll never let me live it down."

He snorted laughter and began kissing her.

Sitting in the library's reading section, idly flipping through magazines, he smiled as he saw Lindsay flit by as she cruised the shelves for a particular book. It had become a habit of theirs to come to this library since coming back to Madison, and Eric had taken to just killing time while she dug around for books she wanted to read.

Eric had always read constantly, and he still wanted to. But his new situation had brought new interests, and until everything was resolved he couldn't afford to garner more questions from Lindsay. It was safer to be patient and wait. Things would fall into place soon enough.

Lindsay's patience had been incredible. She knew there were changes in him, and she knew that there were things that he wasn't telling her yet. Occasionally she would get frustrated and ask, but when he asked her to trust him and wait, she would do so. It troubled him, making her wait and worry, but he saw no other way. He had to reconcile with himself before he could hope to do the same with her.

And in truth, this was all only a minor blemish on what had been months of sheer happiness. It was more than he had ever expected, and certainly more than he felt he deserved. Lindsay was truly happy here with him, and he would do whatever it took to protect that.

When she came walking up with her arms loaded down, he stood to take some from her. She kissed him and grinned. "You didn't find anything?"

"No, not today. Maybe next time."

It was that night he told her that he had to take a trip. He had expected confusion or anger, but to his surprise she just nodded.

"Well, I knew this would come up eventually. This is about the guy in the park, isn't it? Teneber."

Eric nodded. "Yes, at least in part. He's still out there and he's going to come for me. Soon. I want to be far away from you when that happens."

She took in what he said, her dark brown eyes fixed on his own. "Okay. I can understand that. I don't like it, but I understand it. But how do you know he won't come for me instead? Use me against you?"

He shook his head. "First, he wouldn't. It goes against his purpose. I know that doesn't really make sense to you now, but it's true. Second, I can keep you hidden from him. He won't be able to find you, even if you just stay right here in Madison, which you probably should."

Lindsay raised her eyebrow. "Really? You can do that now?"

Looking uncomfortable, Eric nodded. "Um yeah. I can."

Without pausing she went on. "Where will you go?"

"Europe I think. England maybe. Somewhere far away in case things go badly."

She paled, her voice a whisper. "Are they going to go badly?"

He smiled. "No, I don't think so. Everything will work out as it's meant to."

"How long will you be gone?"

His smile faded slightly. "I don't know for sure."

"When do you have to leave?"

"Tomorrow. I should go tomorrow."

Chapter Twenty-Nine

Eric tensed as he stepped off the platform at Paddington station and onto the train, as was his habit when he got on a train these days. He had been in London for three days now, and he had known for the last two that he would meet Teneber on a train. He had no specific knowledge of how or specifically when, but he knew it would be soon.

So it was now his habit to carefully scan the compartment before he entered it and to always find a seat against the front or rear wall so he could see everyone in the compartment. Silly precautions all things considered, but it eased his mind.

Since it had come to him that their meeting would happen on a train, he had started taking day trips by train every day. Yesterday was Dover, and today was Oxford. He knew that it would happen when it happened, and that his whereabouts mattered little in the whole scheme of things, but it gave him something to do.

The train rides themselves were interesting. The one to Dover had been largely empty, but this train was a different story. Mothers with children going back home after a visit to London, business commuters that made the hour-long trip every day, tourists like himself. Seeing the commuters he regretted again that he had not left earlier in the day instead of waiting until late afternoon. As it was, he was going to be spending the night in Oxford and coming back tomorrow. Still, he had enjoyed the time in London as well.

He heard the chime and announcement that the train was leaving the station, followed swiftly by the doors closing with some finality. A couple of seconds passed before he heard a loud rapping on the glass of the door in the vestibule behind his seat. An attendant was near the doors and they were reopened after a moment, allowing the late passenger entry. He didn't need to look up to know it was Teneber who sat down across from him.

"Surprise, Eric! How's your trip going?"

Even after all this time, it seemed that Teneber had a taste for the dramatic, and he seemed somewhat disappointed when Eric looked at him calm and unsurprised.

"Well enough, I guess. How're you?"

Teneber regained from the slip and smiled widely as he gave a shrug. "Can't complain. I've always liked England."

Eric nodded, but didn't say anything else. He'd give Teneber his time to play things out.

Seeing that he wasn't going to respond, Teneber crossed his legs and leaned back in his chair. "It seems that you were expecting me. Secreted the girl away somewhere as well, eh?"

"I had a hunch, yeah."

Teneber nodded. "All very interesting. You've been interesting all along the way. And now it's time for it to all come to an end."

"Yes, I know."

Teneber smiled again, his eyes showing mild surprise. "Are you going to fight it? Fight me?" He uncrossed his legs and leaned forward, watching Eric intently.

Eric shook his head. "No. No, I'm not."

Raising an eyebrow, Teneber's face grew serious. "Very well. A wise choice. Good-bye, Eric." With that he reached out his hand and touched Eric's face. Murmuring in low tones, something passed from him to Eric, sending the final barriers tumbling down.

Leaning back in his seat again, Teneber waited silently for several minutes before speaking. When he did so, it was with a hushed reverence that seemed alien coming from him.

"Hello, Master. Are you well?"

Eric looked at him and nodded. "I'm very well. You've completed the task set before you."

Teneber smiled nervously and nodded again. "Yes, certainly. Have I ever failed to do as you ask?"

Eric looked out the window for a moment, watching the scenery pass by. "No, you never have."

Teneber frowned. "Is something wrong, Master?"

"Wrong? No, not in the way you think of things."

"I'm confused, Master. Aren't you fully restored?"

"I am."

"Excellent, excellent. There was no problem with your Awakening just now, was there?"

Eric turned from the window, looking at Teneber for several seconds before responding. "There was no Awakening just now."

Teneber frowned in confusion. "I don't understand."

"I know you don't. Let me explain. My 'Awakening' as you call it occurred months ago in a dank basement in Illinois. It was then that what you know as the Darkness came forward and recalled what it was. What it had been."

Teneber's face began to draw down into a mask of fury. "You're lying."

"No, actually I'm not. I remembered who and what I was, remembered all of our plans, or at least most of them. It wasn't until you unlocked my full power and knowledge just now that I could remember every single detail. But I recalled enough. I knew of the lie that had been told to me by Raziel, that I was marked for death to bring about an apocalypse. A lie that he fully believed because you had told it to him so convincingly years before.

"I knew that this body was actually meant to be a vessel for my essence in the world, to be my way of exceeding the limitations inherent in dwelling Outside."

"And that would pave the way for you to take over the whole of Creation, and failing that, raze it and start it anew."

Eric sighed. "Yes, that was the idea, wasn't it? A child's idea. A fool's idea."

Teneber, who had begun to calm, looked confused and angry again. "What do you mean?"

Eric leaned forward, looking at Teneber with some sympathy. "Let me tell you a story."

Teneber nodded, still looking uncertain.

Eric sat back and began.

"Once upon a time there was a great being, powerful and vast. So powerful and vast, in fact, that it would be fair to consider it a primal force of existence—one of the many things that made the wheels of Creation turn. But unlike things such as gravity or love, this force had a will of its own. Some would say that such a will and mind were necessary for its work, which was nearly infinite in its complexity and variety. You see, its work was that of pattern and consequence. Of dark deeds and negative probabilities. It was called the Darkness.

"Some would say that was the reason it needed such a will and mind, and perhaps that is so, though I very much doubt it. Whatever the reason, it was granted both and over countless eons it began to desire something more. It well-knew Creation—after all, its reason for being was to manipulate Creation constantly but never be of it. To never truly control it. Over time this frustrated the Darkness, and led to resentment and greed. This led to a plan.

"If it could find a way to bring over its essence into the material world, it could evolve. Become something new, something more. And in time, it could take over and rule all of Creation.

It knew of God, but only as a deep-sea creature has some vague concept of light above the water. This was one of its many flaws you see, for despite all its power and intelligence, all its vast reach and knowledge, it was ignorant of so much that fell outside its narrow existence and its naïve plans. Its thoughts were so alien by human standards as to often be beyond understanding.

"But still its plan looked as if it might work. For centuries it worked, setting things in motion. A frightened boy hiding a knife. A man choosing life over suicide. A monster given a taste of power and devoting his life to regaining it. An angel too proud to ask for forgiveness. And others. So many others. All playing their part in shaping a boy who would be the key to everything.

"And things went according to plan. The boy grew strong and was well-protected. He was pushed and prodded into using the power he had been granted, into slowly opening himself up to that which lay coiled within him.

"Then the boy found himself in a basement, wasted and hopeless, his only thoughts of protecting the world from himself and saving the girl he loved more than anything he had ever known. And in that well of despair, he knelt and prayed. Then he slept. And when he awoke, he had truly Awakened."

Teneber gripped the arms of his chair. "What?"

Eric raised his hand for silence and went on. "For you see, this was not a boy who had been possessed by the Darkness, his own human soul warring against some ancient force. The Darkness *was* his soul. The boy *was* the Darkness.

"Everything that had happened to him, everything he had ever been. The Darkness lived twenty-two years as a boy, the only restriction upon him that of memory. And when he Awakened and regained those memories, do you know what he discovered?"

Teneber swallowed, his face pale. "What?"

"That nothing had changed. As I've said, the Darkness was a very ignorant being for all its power. It knew little of emotion or faith beyond how they could be used to manipulate and destroy. It had no genuine concept of a human existence, or truly of any existence beyond its own.

"But that was no longer the case. It had found a face and a heart. It was Eric Talbot. I *am* Eric Talbot." He extended his hand, a small smile on his face. "Pleased to meet you."

Teneber leapt up from his seat, his voice loud. "You're a damned little liar!"

"You know I'm not."

"Then you've gone insane. You're *pure evil*. You're a *god*. Do you honestly think you're going to just go live as a person now?"

"Sit down." Teneber flushed but sat back down swiftly.

"Now. I'm not insane. Aside from the fact that it is utterly ridiculous that you use the term given that it is a purely human concept, I am fully cognizant of who I am and what I'm doing. Next, I'm not evil. Again, you're using an inexact human term, but this one at least has real weight to it. There is plenty of Evil in this and all levels of reality, but I am and always was simply playing a role in the mechanics of Creation.

"Now, clearly my past plans and reasons for entering this world were evil. Without question. But if you've been paying attention, you realize that we're beyond that embarrassing phase in my development. As for me being a god, that's just silly."

Teneber glared at him. "Do you think I'm going to just smile and swallow this? Where does this leave me? I've served you without pause or question for over three millennia. Do you think you can just cast me aside because you've had some kind of epiphany?"

Eric smiled thinly. "I would like you to accept this, but I know you won't. I made you after all, so I know it's not in your nature, and I have no reason to believe that you've grown in any way in the time since your birth."

Teneber jabbed a finger at him. "Spare me your condescension, boy. Because that's all you are, whatever you've remembered or think you know. Now let me tell you what is going to happen. You're going to do exactly as I say. It's time for you to serve me for a change."

"Or what?"

Teneber gave a smile both genuine and cold. "Or I'll destroy this train and everyone on it."

Chapter Thirty

Eric looked across the aisle to where a small boy was arguing with his mother, his little sister wagging her finger at him and clearly enjoying every second of it. Further down the aisle an old man dozed fitfully, his newspaper continually waking him as it almost slipped from his grasp time and time again. All around were the murmurs of conversations--of lives being lived and plans being made. Eric took it all in and looked back at the small man-thing across from him, its eyes cold and hard, arrogance and triumph carved into every line of its face. And Eric smiled.

"Is that your big move? Threatening a train full of strangers?"

Teneber's expression didn't change. "We both know you don't want their deaths on your head. If you truly are still the boy, that is."

Eric rolled his eyes. "Well no, of course I don't want them to die. But if I had to choose between a couple of hundred people or you gaining the power to eventually destroy the entire world, it's not much of a decision. I mean, did you think this out at all?"

Teneber went on as if Eric hadn't spoken. "How often have you been hurt in your life, boy? Actually physically hurt."

Eric shook his head slightly as he grinned. "Occasionally. Not that often."

"Have you ever been hurt badly?"

"No, of course not. My power naturally prevents that. I know that now, and you always have."

Teneber smiled, raising a finger. "Ah. Quite so. And yet....the old man, Hobbes. *He* hurt you didn't he? Hurt you quite badly in fact....when he bit your shoulder. Choked you as well if my memory serves." He tipped a wink. "And it does."

Eric nodded, frowning slightly at the memory. "Yes, he did. A side effect of his prior contact with my power."

Teneber actually chuckled now, his eyes dancing. "You know, I thought the same thing at first. But then I came up with a better answer."

"And that would be...?"

Smiling beatifically, Teneber spread his hands like a magician beginning a trick. "This."

Teneber's hand was a blur--Eric did not see its actions, but somehow *knew* what was occurring nonetheless. In the breath between seconds, the knife appeared in Teneber's hand. The knife that had killed Hobbes, covered in the same symbols that had adorned the monster's metal teeth. The knife he had left down in the cave in his rush to save Lindsay.

In one flowing movement, Teneber gripped the knife firmly and slammed it into the middle of Eric's chest.

Lindsay was in the basement of the library when she passed out. She had taken on the volunteer job two days after Eric had left, unable to bear the empty days without something to occupy her time. The library had seemed like the most natural choice, and she had enjoyed the work so far, even if it did get monotonous at times. This morning she was going through stacks of donated old books to pick out those that they would keep and those that they would send on to the state distribution center. The best part of the job was that she had been told she could pick out books for herself as she went.

She was thumbing through a children's book about an aardvark that wanted to become a knight when she felt her throat tightening. The room tilted around her as she reached for the walls and found them strangely distant. Images flashed through her mind--children, seats, and the man from the park. She gasped as she realized who it was she was seeing and what it all may mean.

It's happening. It's happening right now, and oh God, why did I let him go without me oh oh what does it mean why am I seeing this why didn't I make him stay and protect him OH GOD what's happening to him...

She took a step forward and stumbled, hitting a wall and leaning against it for support as she pushed herself away and tried again. She had to try to help, as pointless as it would be.

But the images and dizziness continued to assail her as she tried to walk again. Her vision wavering, she tried to sit down, thought better of it, and then pitched forward as her consciousness fled.

Eric looked down at Teneber's hand and then looked back up, his eyes distant. "You know, a few months ago that would have killed me. But as you can see," He pulled Teneber's hand away as he spoke, the crude pommel of the knife's hilt smooth where the blade had shattered as it touched Eric, "That is no longer the case. I've had some time to gain control of things. Still, it was a nice little idea you had, if a bit obvious."

Teneber stood, flinging down the hilt. "You've "gained control of things"? All that meat and bone has driven you insane. You have no concept of your power. Not as you are. And not in this place." His lips skinned back from his teeth as he screamed, several passengers looking frightened and the mother across the aisle moving her children to the other end of the car and beyond. "*This is not your place. It's* mine. You've had a few months to gain control of the paltry powers you had access to before today? I've had over three millennia to master mine. Three millennia I spent *serving you.*"

Eric sighed and nodded. "I know this. Just as I know that you won't stop no matter what I do or say. Not unless I make you."

Teneber spit, the liquid sizzling on the metal armrest beside Eric where it landed. Wiping his mouth with the back of his hand, the man stepped out into the aisle. "I tire of this. Time to start killing."

Eric shook his head slowly. "Not quite time, no."

Teneber looked around, fear slipping around the edges of his mask for a moment before he regained his composure. They were standing in the middle of a field, the wind-blown waves of green grass interrupted only by a large tree nearby and a low stone fence some distance behind them. He cut his eyes to Eric, his gaze full of hate.

"*What did you do?*"

Eric looked around, taking in a deep breath of air. "I brought us to Wales. I'm pretty sure this is Wales at least."

The little man ground his teeth as his eyes burned in his head. "I know *where* we are, boy. But *how* did you do it?"

Eric's eyes narrowed slightly. "I can do all manner of things now. This wasn't hard."

Teneber struck without another word, his fiery gaze intent upon Eric as he lashed out at him across several levels, lines of energy and magic darting and weaving their way across the distance. Eric saw them all and pushed them back, holding them until Teneber let them fade. Teneber tried twice more, stronger each time, both with the same result. The man-thing was feeling him out. Testing him.

"You've got a great deal of power, Teneber. And I can see that you've been busy with more than dealing with *my* affairs in your time on earth. Some of this power didn't come from me."

The little man grinned savagely. "I've always believed in having contingency plans." He struck out again, with such force and savagery that Eric was forced to take a step back, the shockwave from the impact shattering the nearby tree and sending portions of the stone fence behind them into collapse.

Teneber laughed. "Not quite as omnipotent as you act, eh? Still have a few things to learn?"

Eric shook his head. "I've never been all-powerful. And yes, I'm still learning. Still becoming whatever I'm meant to be."

The little man shorted. "What you're meant to be? You were a Shaper of the All, a Weaver of Destiny. And you've fallen this low? How disappointing. How *pathetic.* At least the angel had spine."

"I don't expect you to understand. You can't. You can't change or evolve. You were always the best at what you did, but that's all you ever were. A tool."

"Spare me."

Eric looked at Teneber sadly. "I should know, Teneber. I made you." He lowered his head. "I made you too well. And not well enough."

The man glared at Eric, the air crackling between them. "What does that mean?"

Eric looked back up, raising his hand. "That I can't save you. That you don't serve a purpose any more. And that your time is done. Good-bye, Mr. Teneber."

The energy in the air died suddenly as Teneber began to rot away before his eyes, the wind carrying away pieces of him until there was nothing left. Eric watched the process in silence, a solemn look upon his face. When it was done, he looked up at the sky, slowly filling with brilliant oranges and purples as sunset approached. Eric studied the sky for several minutes before he nodded and began walking away. Then he was gone.

Epilogue

Eric stepped into the room quietly, watching the gentle rise and fall of Lindsay's sleeping breaths for several minutes before stepping up to the hospital bed. Brushing her hair out of her face, he kissed her forehead softly.

Her eyes fluttered twice and then came open, growing large as they focused upon him. He almost laughed at the look of surprise on her face.

"Eric? Oh, God...Are you okay?"

He nodded, pulling a chair near and sitting down beside her. "I am. But thanks for the vote of confidence. From the look on your face you thought I was dog food." He did laugh now, giving her hand a squeeze.

Tears started trickling from the corners of her eyes. "I saw...I saw that something was happening to you. That you were in danger. I...must have passed out." She looked around the hospital room, noticing it for the first time. "Who brought me here?"

"I did. This morning. You hadn't been found yet when I got to you, so I brought you to the ER right away to get you checked out."

Confusion spread across her face as he spoke. "Did I bump my head or something? I thought you were in England."

He grinned at her. "You did bump your head, though you'll be fine. But you're right. I was. I came back when I was finished with Teneber. I brought myself back."

She looked at him for several seconds before nodding. "Um, okay. Apparently I've missed a lot." She squeezed his hand back, holding onto it desperately. "But the only thing that matters is that you're back and that you're okay."

He nodded and leaned over to kiss her. The entire time he had been in England he had known he had missed Lindsay terribly, but it wasn't until he was back with her that he truly understood the depth of it. Kissing her long and deep, he finally forced himself to pull back, his face more serious.

"Teneber is gone. Permanently. And I've got a lot to tell you when we get you home, which should be in a couple of more hours."

She nodded, raising an eyebrow at his tone. "Should I be scared?"

Eric smiled weakly. "I don't think so. No, I know you shouldn't. But...well, there's just a lot to tell."

When they reached home, Eric wanted to know if she wanted anything to eat before they talked, but she refused the offer, knowing that she couldn't possibly enjoy anything (or likely even keep it down) until the cold fishes stopped churning in her belly. And that wouldn't happen until they talked. If they stopped then.

So they sat down and Eric began telling what he had done since he had left her—of places he had been and things he had done. She knew that he was nervous, and that telling her these trivial things was his way of working up to what really mattered, so she just sat and took it all in until he reached his train ride to Oxford.

But as soon as he mentioned Teneber's arrival, he went back to the day before he had rescued her from Hobbes, a day he had spent in the basement of that terrible house as he had the days before. He told her about praying and the sleep that followed. About waking up and all that he remembered.

She flinched slightly as he told this, the words pouring out of him in a torrent now, and she forced herself to stay steady, telling herself that he was still Eric and that everything was going to be all right.

When he was done explaining about himself, he went back to his encounter with Teneber, not pausing to give her any chance to respond. He pushed on through their conversation, the knife, the journey to Wales, and all that followed, including finding her in the basement of the library. When he was finished, Eric leaned back in his seat and watched her, his lips pale and his eyes frightened.

She nearly jumped with surprise when she heard herself speaking.

"So you're still Eric? *Really really* Eric?"

He nodded. "Really really Eric. I'm still who I was."

She shook her head slightly. "But still...how can you be? Now that you know that you're this...thing, this Darkness. How does that work?"

He sighed. "Lindsay, I am the Darkness. But the thing you have to realize is that I spent eons as a blank slate in a lot of ways. I had no emotions aside from a few base desires, and while I had intelligence, it wasn't human intelligence. I had no heart or soul."

She lowered her eyes. "And you do now?"

Lindsay could feel him tense without looking up. "I guess that's for you to decide."

Looking out the window, her vision swam as her eyes brimmed with tears. "I'll need some time."

Eric stood up. "Okay. I'll give it to you." Without waiting for a further response, he walked out of the room, and a moment later she heard the front door shut.

The heartbeat of the world, of all of Creation, thudded softly in Eric's ears as he walked along the city streets, his senses alive in ways they never had been before. He could see and feel and *do* so much now, and he knew that he still had a great deal to learn. But all of that would come later. Even that heartbeat, pulsing with an elegant and glorious beauty that caught his breath in his throat, mattered little to him at the moment. Not when his heart fluttered like a frightened bird in his chest and his mouth seemed to be filled with ashes. Not when he might lose Lindsay.

He returned home two hours later, unable to stay away any longer. When he saw that Lindsay was gone and that there was a note from her on the table, his stomach dropped. It took him a moment to steady his hand enough to read the note, and when he did, he wasn't sure what to make of it. It said:

Eric,
Come to the old farmhouse we looked at before Raziel caught up with us. Use the old-fashioned way to travel, okay?

Lindsay

He folded the note and stuck it in his back pocket. They had never stayed here long enough to get cell phones, so he had no way to reach her aside from following her instructions. No way that he would risk using at least, not with her asking him to drive out there instead of just going to her. Sighing, he left the apartment again and caught a taxi to the same car rental place they had used before. He made it just before they closed, the woman behind the counter clearly surly at being bothered. But despite this, he was out on the road ten minutes later, flying along until he drew near the church, his pace slowing as he passed by.

Soon he was at the house, the black SUV they had taken from Raziel parked out front and a green pickup truck leaving as he drove up. The man behind the wheel had given him a friendly wave as they passed, and Eric gave a half-hearted response as he pulled the car to a stop and got out.

Lindsay was on the front porch, her face unsmiling as she came down the steps to him. He felt his heart lurch.

"I've had time to think about everything."

He nodded. "And?"

"Well, I've got a couple of questions."

"Sure. Sure. Go ahead."

She looked up at him, her eyes deep and her face beautiful as dusk came on. "First, if you were this big force in Creation, aren't you kind of going to be missed?"

He smiled slightly and shook his head. "No. It's kind of hard to explain, but I'm still there doing that. Part of me is anyway. It's kind of automatic--at least now it is."

She frowned slightly but nodded. "Okay. Next question. Now that you know who you are, what do you want from life?"

He didn't pause. "You. I want you. I know I'll get a lot more than that, maybe a lot that I don't want, but all of that's still uncertain. At least to me. But the one thing I know without question is that I love you and I want to be with you always."

She turned away from him, looking back at the house. The silence stretched out between them, Eric becoming increasingly aware of the crickets chirruping in the grass and the sighing wind as it buffeted the fireflies that were beginning to appear. Then she spoke.

"This house. I just bought it. That was the realtor leaving just now. It's going to take some work, but I think it'll make a good place." She turned back to him, and he could see that her cheeks were wet with tears. She went to him, hugging him tightly. "Eric, I don't care about anything that's happened. I don't care who or what you were. I know you now, and I know your heart. You are the truest, best person that I've ever known, and I love you." Her voice began to break. "So much."

He looked down at her, his head swimming as he began to smile. "Lindsay, I.."

She shook her head. "One more question."

He fell silent and nodded.

She looked up at him, her eyes still serious. "Will you marry me?"

Eric laughed. "Of course I will." He bent down to kiss her, their breaths mingling as he held her close. They swayed together, both of them laughing and crying, the dulcet music of Creation singing to Eric as they moved. It seemed as natural as breathing when they began to dance in the fading light, the yellow flicker of the fireflies floating around them like a dream. They were a long time waking.

About the Author

Brandon Faircloth lives in the southern United States and has loved a good story since he was born...especially the scary ones. Look for more of his works in ebook format and print, as well as various places on the internet such as r/nosleep and r/verastahl. For updated news or to contact him, please visit Verastahl.com.

Made in the USA
Middletown, DE
30 November 2023

44002166R00103